The

VAMPIRE

and the

Highland Empath

Clover Autrey

Published by Red Rover Books
Cover art by Pat Autrey
Photos used to design cover were legally obtained from
Dreamstime.com

ISBN- 1477641262

ISBN-13: 978-1477641262

HIGHLAND SORCERY NOVELS

HIGHLAND SORCERER

THE VAMPIRE AND THE HIGHLAND EMPATH

HIGHLAND SHAPESHIFTER

HIGHLAND MOONSIFTER

THE EAGLEKIN SERIES

UPON EAGLE'S LIGHT

CHASE THE WIND

FALLEN WARRIOR

OTHER BOOKS BY CLOVER AUTREY

SEA BORN

THE SWEETHEART TREE

I have many people to thank for
The Vampire and the Highland Empath.

To Pat and the boys for letting me drag them to the
Scottish Festival and Highland Games on a hot, windy
Saturday in Texas.

My wonderful critique partners, the Cowtown Critiquers,
who are always willing to pull out the cattle prod during
brain-storming sessions. I so enjoy getting together with
you guys.

And to my fabulous editor, Melodee Curtis. This wouldn't
be nearly as good without your feedback and ability of
getting to the heart of what really matters. I adore that you
waaaaaay overthink things.

Hugs to you all.

The Vampire and the Highland Empath

Scotland, May 5, 1941

It felt like stepping into a tomb. Yet the woman laid out upon the stone slab was hardly dead.

She'd merely slept through the last seven centuries while nations crumbled and were reformed around her.

The darkness of the cavern was oppressive, the air stale. Outside, waves pounded the cliffs, rumbling through the enclosing stone like the pulse of a waking beast, its breath heavy with salt from the sea air that blew inside the cave. A place that had been forgotten, left untouched and spelled for nearly a thousand years.

Roque could hardly believe he found it. Found her.

More fable than legend.

A beloved sister, hidden away by a grief-stricken brother within the farthest fold inside an ancient smugglers nest. The recessed cavern hidden and all within was presented by an undying spell that humans would see and feel only as solid rock, never knowing the priceless treasure slumbering on the other side of illusion.

Yet Roque was far from human.

His preternatural eyes saw through the magic. Nor was the enclosing darkness a factor.

He made out slender arms crossed over slow rising and falling breasts, enclosed in pristine white fabric. His blood hungered, rising to the surface as it discerned the low hum of the woman's pulse, sluggish in sleep. The predator in him surged to the surface, recognizing easy prey.

Roque froze, calming the beast within himself. *She is not yours for the taking.*

Oh, but he wanted to. Beads of sweat broke out across his brow. His fingers curled at his sides, arms rigid. With one waft of the sleeper's potent blood, impulses he'd strived years to keep under control roiled through him, making Roque feel once again weak-willed and out of control. His own feral blood roared to meet hers, to consume, to take all.

Vampire.

Monster.

No. He could be one without the other. He was strong enough to fight his urges. Had been strong enough for years.

With practiced exertion, he forced the rapid monster within back to the shadows like a lion tamer utilizing a whip.

Back. Back.

Ever watchful of the beast ready to pounce, he could never turn away from what slept in his blood.

He uncurled his fists. Found his calm. Ignored the hunger that throbbed through his veins. He had a job to do.

Whether this worked or not, the spell of illusion and the sleeper's resting place would be destroyed. With one step, Roque passed through the barrier of hidden magic. Charged energy hissed across his skin, lifting the ends of his hair.

Just like that, the spell preserving the woman's body—keeping her from aging, keeping her alive—disintegrated.

Even a spell as powerful as this withered beneath the force of that which sang through Roque's blood.

She would have to be awakened now. Or die.

Which for the purpose Roque had come here, might be the less dangerous outcome for everyone.

His burden. His fault.

He moved into the back of the caves, a silent wraith.

His blood surged as he neared the altar, reaching outward, hungering for the magic it sensed.

The creature within him was damn near salivating.

Which shouldn't be happening. He had tamed the beast long ago.

He looked down upon her and his pulse flared for an entirely different reason.

By gods. Legend had spoken of her loveliness, but Roque had dismissed it as fanciful embellishments of the bespelled slumbering beauty.

Legend had no idea.

She looked as though she had fallen asleep only hours ago. Her smooth skin still retained a healthy blush. Dark lashes fanned over high cheekbones. Soft waves of hair spread across the quilt someone, most likely her brother, had placed beneath her head. Even in the darkness, he could see it was the color of deep crimson sunset.

His hand moved of its own volition to hover above her cheek, run his thumb upon petal-soft lips.

The beast growled to be released, his blood scalding beneath his flesh.

Magic pulsed upon the air—pure and undiluted with darkness.

In all the decades he'd survived, he'd never felt magic so pristinely untouched.

Take it. Take it. Clean your soul.

He stumbled back, horrified at the temptation rising up into his throat.

He could do it. He could succumb to the urges of the beast. His gaze dropped back to the woman, her serene features, her softly rising and falling chest, and he could not destroy her.

She had to live.

However, it was possible that by evaporating the spell she had been cocooned within, he had just signed her death warrant.

Roque took a deep breath, steadying himself for what he was about to attempt.

"Alex, I hope you know what you're talking about," he spoke to the shadows. It was a longshot at best. Her brother, the most powerful wizard known to history, had not been able to awaken her, what chance did a vampire from the lower east side of London have?

You're more than that, the beast inside his blood hissed, restless. Eager. *You're the only one who can do it.*

Roque leaned over the woman and smoothed back her hair with a tenderness he didn't know he still possessed. Soft as silk.

"Wake up, Sleeping Beauty."

Snaking an arm beneath her shoulders, he lifted her—

—and plunged his teeth into the vulnerable hollow of her neck.

Ecstasy flooded his veins. He hadn't tasted blood in so long, the beast fully awoke. Hungry. So hungry.

Her blood was warm, sweet as honey, filling his mouth and throat as he drank. Power vibrated beneath his skin, ancient magic from when the world was young, before the darkness consumed the land and awoke creatures older than time that never should have been awakened.

Her magic sang, burned, scorched his throat. Had he been human, the rush of her magic would scald him, searing from the inside out.

Yet he was more than human.

More even than vampire.

The creature that lay within him was more ancient than that.

Which is why he was here, the only one who stood a whisper's chance of shocking the woman out of her deep slumber. He felt the shift in himself, the stirrings of transformation, the cracking of bone and sinew. No!

Recalling his purpose, Roque slammed down upon his beast and quit drawing from the girl's blood and magic, though it was the hardest thing he'd done in decades, leaving him overwhelmed and afraid.

He'd damned near lost control.

The beast roared, unsated.

Roque pushed back, breathing heavily, his lungs still on fire, his teeth still in the woman's tender neck tissue.

The urge to take and take and take throbbed through his body.

He never lost control, couldn't afford to. Never loosened the hold he had on the beast, yet, with one taste of this girl's magic . . . gods.

Shaken to the core, he reined in every ounce of will he had left...

. . . and gave.

Connected by flesh, mouth upon neck, connected by blood and magics. Roque tapped into that ancient part of himself. Tapped into the beast, the dragon, and let his magic pour through him. He released that overpowering dark force within his blood that he dared never touch upon, into the girl, hoping Alex had not been wrong. Also hoping the man had not underestimated Roque's ability to pull the dragon back once it was loose.

He was afraid.

The dragon stormed past his barriers, vaporous jaws stretched to engulf the woman's essence.

No.

Roque clawed at the serpent, torn. The dragon's magic could awaken her... but it could also kill.

Flame erupted from his fingers. Horrified, Roque flinched back, dropping the girl back upon her bed of quilts. Blood stained her neck. The quilts caught fire.

Bloody hell. Roque pulled back on the dragon. Hard. Forced it away and the flames flickering off his hands extinguished.

He grabbed the woman up into his arms, patting out the fire that caught the edge of her frilly sleeve.

The woman convulsed in his arms. Her eyes flashed open.

Green. Intensely green.

From deathly asleep to fully alert in seconds.

Roque went utterly still.

The girl stared back at him and then took in the burning coverings on the stone altar, the dark cavern walls. Her brows pulled together in confusion and her gaze focused back on him.

She shoved against his chest. "Where are my brothers? Who are you?"

Her voice held the deep lilt of the Scottish Highlands and held him enthralled. He'd expected a dry rasp from disuse, but the spell that surrounded her for centuries had preserved her well. No aging, no need for sustenance, no atrophy of muscle tone. It was as though she'd slept minutes instead of nearly a thousand years. Even the quilts and her clothing had remained untouched by time.

She shoved at him again, squirming to get out of his hold. Her tone hitched with rising panic. "Where are my brothers? Where's Charity?"

Roque's response was to grip her more tightly and head toward the adjoining cavern.

"Let me down." She twisted out of his arms, forcing

Roque to stumble forward to keep her from hitting the rocky ground. He snagged her waist and pulled her to him so her face wouldn't hit stone.

She froze against him.

Slowly she twisted around to study him, her eyes wide. His extraordinary reflexes made her re-evaluate who he was. *What* he was.

Her body shifted away. Her wariness hurt. It shouldn't matter to him, but it hurt. She cupped her neck, brought her hand down and stared at the blood on her fingers. Dark brows drew together as she glared up at him, accusation hard in her eyes.

He let her go.

She backed away. "Get away from me. Who are you?" Her hands fluttered to her waist, undoubtedly searching for a blade she must have once kept there.

Roque glanced toward the fire on the altar. Smoke was filling the room, but the flames would be out soon with nothing left to burn. "You want to stay here?"

She flinched. Her eyes traveled to the low light spilling in from the adjacent cave and the only way out of the smugglers hideout. She would have to get past him.

"Ye're English?" Her eyes tightened, seeing him instantly as the enemy from his accent.

He sighed. "I'm here to help you." It suddenly seemed critical that she believe him. He frowned. Her trust wasn't necessary. It'd be nothing to carry her out by force, but his every nerve jumped around inside him as she stared into his face. He had the vague impression she could uncover what was left of his tattered soul.

One eye squinted as though she could see him better that way. Perhaps she couldn't see him well at all with the smoke and the darkness. She would not have the keen eyesight of his kind.

Her fingers scrabbled at the folds of her gown. "Are my brothers outside? Is this. . . ." She glanced around. "Is this the Shadowrood?"

His mouth went dry. The mention of the otherworld of the Fae made his blood run cold. "No."

She jerked and he immediately regretted his harsh tone. After all, she knew nothing of what her family had done. She couldn't know that her brothers had destroyed the world.

Chapter Two

Roque extended his hand. "I'll tell you everything once we're out of here. It's not safe."

He wasn't looking forward to explaining that everyone she'd ever known, everything she'd ever known, were gone. And there was no way he was saying anything now, not without knowing how she'd react. She could run, not that he couldn't catch her. Or worse, go into hysterics.

Though he had to admit she was taking waking up in unfamiliar surroundings fairly well. Of course, she had no inkling of how much time had passed during her slumber.

Her chin set and her eyes glinted. Roque stared, transfixed by her abrupt change in demeanor.

"Ye'll tell me now." She came to him, lifting her palm to his chest.

Empath.

The last of her kind. Roque remained perfectly still, tamping down the urge to swipe her hand away and close himself off. He did not want the ugly contents of his life bared to her. He was not a good man. He had done things.

Murderer.

Yet he wanted her trust. His gaze flitted to the blood

on her neck.

Magic arrowed into his chest—powerful and old, the likes he'd never felt, and he had experienced a lot.

The woman's features scrunched together, devastated. She looked less the fierce empath and more little girl lost. "What's wrong?"

"I . . . ?" Her palm slipped from him, taking the warmth of her magic.

Roque caught her hand. "Whatever it is, you can trust me."

"Can I?" Her words snagged on a cry. She covered the bloody pricks on her neck with her palm.

"You . . . ? He startled. "You don't know?"

Her eyes swept over him like an accusation.

"I know what you are," he admitted.

Her lips trembled.

He sensed her pulse speeding up. Roque narrowed his gaze, unsure of what she saw in him. *Monster. Beast.* "You know that you can trust me."

"I do not know." She pressed her palms to her head. It hurt to hear that. "I cannot . . . I could not feel anything." Her eyes lifted to his, wet and pleading. A punch to his gut.

Roque stared down at her, seeing the truth of it in her eyes. Every nerve inside of him loosened. Panicked laughter bubbled up inside his throat—a cosmic joke.

Hitler's long unattained weapon—an empath able to uncover all plots and enemies against the *Führer*—

useless.

Roque's lips curled. Fate had just made his job of keeping this particular weapon out of the Nazi's hands that much easier.

Except . . . the devastation paling the empath's face shot straight to his heart. He understood what losing a part of your soul felt like.

"Edeen," he whispered her name finally. He hadn't meant for it to echo around the stone like a prayer in a great cathedral.

She flinched back. The firelight flickered around the interior, reflecting within those lovely haunted eyes.

"Come outside with me." He again offered his hand. "I promise I'll help you. We'll figure this out." The thought of her being tested and examined even by the Allied scientists brought a bad taste to his mouth. "Trust me."

She frowned, delicate brows drawing downward. She'd probably never had to trust anyone without sensing their true intentions before. Roque held himself very still, unnerved by how badly he wanted her trust.

She slid her palm against his and Roque's world tilted sideways. He nodded, his throat tight. Folding her smaller hand within his own, Roque guided Edeen through the outer cave, past old broken and looted crates and out onto the slender sea-drenched ledge forty feet above the slashing waves. The cliff wall extended another thirty feet above them. The wind slapped the rope he'd used to climb down to the smugglers cave upon the rocks.

Muted sunlight filtered down through clouds heavy with approaching rain. The reptile in him preened. Had he wings, the dragon would stretch them to soak up the sun. Roque grinned, counting this one thing regarding the mixture of his heritage a blessing. He was the only vampire in existence immune to the terminal effects of sunlight.

In fact, his dragon side craved it.

He detected the woman's gaze on him and turned to her. Again, he was struck by her beauty. In the light she became a riot of colors. Creamy skin, rose-tinted lips. Vibrant intelligent eyes the shade of verdant green. And her hair, a deep auburn with interwoven streaks of brighter copper and honey browns.

Treasure. The beast inside flicked open its eye for a closer look.

She was looking at him warily. "I know this place. Magby's Cove. Why are we here?"

Your brother hid you away. He did not want to tell her any of this. With a few words he'd be taking everything she once knew from her. *But he'd promised her.* His voice tangled around his throat like a noose.

"Edeen, you've been asleep—"

"Roquemore Giordano," a voice called from the cliffs above.

Roque stiffened, craning his head upward. He'd know

20

that voice in his worst nightmares. Wulf.

From above, *Sturmhauptführer* Wulf Geschopf of the bloody SS leaned over the edge of the cliff. If only a strong gust would topple him over. Several men were with him, in civilian clothing, high-necked sweaters and jackets, though their close cropped hair and straight bearing marked them as soldiers of the *Schutzstaffel*. As did the Kar 98k rifles pointing down at them. Perfect, Geschopf brought bloody members of the bloody SS with him.

Into Scotland. Enemy territory. The *Sturmhauptführer* had large ones, he'd give him that.

Roque guided Edeen out of view beneath the lips of the cavern. "I didn't expect to see you here," he called up conversationally. Where the bleeding hell was Alex? He'd left him up top as watch. If Geschopf had harmed the young man . . . ."

"I would not expect so." Geschopf peeled off a glove. "But then I always manage to catch you off-guard, don't I, Roquemore? You know freedom's such a fleeting promise. I'll always be able to find you. Whenever I want to find you." He stretched out his fingers, cracking knuckles as claws grew out from his fingertips.

Roque's heart beat crazily at the implications. Geschopf must have known where he was all this time. And he'd led him straight to the empath. He'd let Roque awaken her before springing his trap. The bastard had played him.

A tremor rolled through Roque, The ghostly jab of needles prickled his veins. Electrical jolts seared every nerve. Experimented upon. Caged. The dragon nearly unchained and never quite the same again.

He wouldn't go back to Geschopf's cage.

Light fingers curled over his arm. He looked down at Edeen. He wouldn't let that be her fate either.

"Who is that man?" she whispered.

Butcher.

Scientist.

The Führer*'s Hunter, known by reputation as Die Schwarzen Klaue. The Black Claw.*

"No one you should ever have to know."

"He is a cruel man."

Roque's head whipped upward again. "Can you sense—?"

"Nay. I see the cruelty in the planes of his face." She scanned about for a way out, eyeing the rope that dangled past them and then below at the treacherous rocks angling up out of the foaming swells. "What are we going to do?"

Roque smiled at the steel in her spine.

"Do you trust me?"

She canted her head toward the cliff wall. "More than him."

That would have to do.

Geschopf kicked at the rope with the toe of his boot, flicking it outward. "Climb up, Roquemore. Send the girl first. Or does she need assistance?"

Anger flashed across Edeen's brow. Wind pushed her hair in front of her face and she grabbed it and held it back.

Roque motioned her back inside the cave.

They went all the way back to the stone slab. The bottom of her gown swept across the stone floor. All that remained of the quilts were soot and ash.

Edeen placed her hands on her hips. "You have a plan."

"That I do." One he was certain she was not going to like.

"Well, what is—"

He didn't give her a chance to ask. Or object. Racing forward, he grabbed her up and sprinted toward the wide opening. With a running leap, he hurtled off the ledge. He was faster, stronger than a normal man and hoped that his extra last push helped them clear the rocks below.

They plunged downward. Wind whipped across them.

Bullets shrieked past.

Geschopf cried. "Cease firing. *Feuer einstellen.* I don't want them hit!"

Too late.

White sharp pain speared down Roque's side. He curled tighter around the woman and hit the sea like a torpedo.

Chapter Three

Edeen came up sputtering, the man, Roquemore, kicking to the surface with her.

"Can you swim?" He pulled her closer.

"Ye ask me now?" She knew she should never trust an Englishman.

His eyes crinkled until his gaze went beyond her and his lips thinned. "Shite."

Twisting, Edeen saw the man from the cliff dive and slice into the water as cleanly as an arrow. He'd jumped after them?

Both men were clearly insane.

Nor human, of that she was certain. It'd take someone—gifted, of otherworldly abilities—to propel themselves (and her with him) far enough out to clear the rocks.

Another man jumped from the cliff. Then two more. All more than mortals apparently.

Roquemore pulled her through the water, edging along the cliffs. Edeen tried to keep up. She was a strong swimmer, but did not have anywhere near the speed as the man hauling her through the waves. The muscles in his arms bunched and lengthened near her side. She tried to kick around the long folds of her gown tangling in her legs.

A hand clamped around her ankle, hauling her under.

The man, the one who jumped after them—Wulf?—his face was a white orb in the inky water. An iron grip flung around her arm, spinning her. He pulled her away.

Edeen jerked her arms to break loose, but the man had a strong grip. Pressure filled her lungs. Bubbles poured from his nose, streaming to the surface. Her gown puffed around them like a drifting cloud, hampering them both as they sank like anchor stones. The man remained calm, didn't seem to care he was drowning, or her with him.

A dark form streaked toward them. Roque came at them, dark hair streaming. Angry. Determined. Fierce.

He pounced on Wulf, pushing them down. Edeen's arm wrenched, dragged with them. Until suddenly she was yanked free, spiraling loose in the water. Spots danced before her vision. A great crowding pressure clamped her muscles tight, lungs screaming. She had to breathe.

Kicking toward the surface, she tugged the heavy skirt around her hips, freeing her legs.

The men were a tangled hazy twisting mass below her. She kicked and kicked and broke free of the surface just as she lost all her air.

Floundering, she sucked in a painful gasp, nearly choking it down into pain-riddled lungs. She would never breathe right again.

A boat raced toward her, the likes of which she couldn't fathom. She had never seen a vessel cut through the water so swiftly, especially without oars or sail.

It pulled up noisily alongside her and a young man leaned over the side, arm extended. "Grab on, Miss."

Still heaving air into her lungs, Edeen pushed away from the strange little boat. It's back end rattled and rumbled, smoke curling from an odd iron monster, making all the noise. The man in the boat must be a powerful sorcerer to tame such a beast.

"Ma'am, please. I'm here to help."

Which could be true or nay. Whatever his intent 'twould be preferable to staying within the freezing sea. Also escaping one lone young man would be simpler than escaping the many magic wielders who'd jumped in after her. Bluidy mercenaries, Col would say of them.

An ache pierced her heart at the thought of her youngest brother and what might have befallen him. The last she remembered was Aldreth the witch attacking her family on Crunfathy Hill.

The man in the boat still held his hand out to her. She would go with him mayhap, but not without Roque.

A wave carried her closer to the thin hull and she panicked. Taking a short breath, she dove back under. She couldn't see anything and her heart took a sudden dip.

Chest tight, she dove down farther, hoping to find him.

Something grabbed her behind the shoulders and hauled upward. She broke the surface again, kicking and fighting. "Let go! Let me be."

Strong arms pulled her in close. "What were you doing?"

Roque? She stilled in his arms, blinking water out of her eyes. A wave splashed over them both. When it cleared, she squinted against the salt water. "I was going to help you."

The hard line of his lips softened. "Well. . . ." He sloughed back his wet hair. "I had it handled. Get in the boat. Alex." He practically shoved her up into the waiting arms where the young man hauled her over the side, hitting the cross seat on her back.

"Welcome aboard, ma'am."

Roque rolled inside, shouting, "For the love of God and country, Alex, get us out of here."

The boat tipped and a clawed hand curled over the side. Roque spun, kicking at it.

"Is that?" Alex paled.

"Go!" Roque slammed his heel down on the scaly fingers and the boat lurched to life, its nose lifting and crashing back onto a crest of a wave as it charged forward.

Alex fought the snarling, smoking iron beast tethered

to the back of the boat, hands clasped around some sort of a rod that he steered the little monster with.

Edeen rolled to her stomach. Roque kicked again and the claw-hand lost its grip. The Wulf rolled away in a swath of spray.

Roque knelt by her and shouted above the little beast's roar. "You all right?"

"Roque!" Alex shouted from behind and pointed with the hand not taming the noisy monster. "You've been hit."

Both Roque and Edeen followed his gaze to a patch of crimson seeping through the side of Roque's shirt.

He pulled the wet material away to finger a small hole.

"Huh."

Chapter Four

"He stabbed you?" Edeen grabbed onto Roque's shirt where he knelt, pulling it up for a better look. She didn't recall seeing a knife. The hard muscles of his stomach flinched. She found the bleeding wound on his heated side and pressed her hand against it.

Alex pulled the boat to a sliding stop and came over, his face creased with little lines of worry.

"Keep going," Roque snarled. "We need to get her out of here. Did you see who that was?"

"I saw." A muscle in Alex's jaw ticked. "I saw when they came onto the road at the top of the cliffs. I had just enough time to scramble out of there and secure this magnificent craft." He spread his arms wide. "You're welcome, by the way. Now let me see how bad and then I'll save your hide for the second time today."

Roque's lips hitched upward and he spread his arms to let the young man get at the wound.

Alex gaped at Edeen's hand on Roque. "Ma'am?"

She wasn't ready to relinquish her hold. 'Twas foolish, but she felt as though she was the only thing keeping the man's lifeblood inside. "Are ye a healer?"

Both men looked at her askance. Alex bobbed his head. Water droplets flicked off his blond hair. "No, ma'am, I've not the gift, but I've had field training."

Edeen searched his face. 'Twas difficult without her gift to know what to believe. He seemed sincere, though much of that could be due to his youthful innocent appearance. But he had already plucked them from the sea and Roque seemed to trust him. She bristled at the unbidden thought, wondering why that should matter when she didn't know if Roque himself was someone she could trust. Her neck throbbed. He had done something to her after all.

She withdrew her palms from his circular wound though she leaned in for a better look at Alex's probing.

Roque sucked in a hiss when Alex spread the skin around the wound. More blood poured out.

"So that was him?" Alex said. "Geschopf."

"In the flesh." Roque clenched his jaw. His pallor was graying. "Or whatever. He won't be far behind us in securing his own boat. Are you satisfied? Can we go now?"

Alex wiped his hands on his thighs. "You'll live."

Roque snorted like it was a jest.

Edeen replaced her hands over Roque's wound. "He needs a healer." She turned on him. "Take me to my brothers. A healer travels with them."

Something indefinable shifted behind Roque's eyes. A strange look passed between the men. Edeen stilled.

Unease sank into her heart.

"We've no time for that." Alex took his place back near the smoking little beast. "We've wasted enough as it is."

"You wasted," Roque muttered.

The boat rocked on a swell. Edeen started ripping at the hem of her underskirts. Why was she in this finery anyway? She hadn't been wearing this on the hill by their village. And where were her belt and dirk?

The boat lunged forward again. Anticipating it, Roque grabbed her arms to steady her.

She met his gaze. "Ye're losing too much blood. D'ye not care?"

"I have enough to spare."

His indifference to his own well-being made her angry. She pressed the torn cloth to his side. "I do not understand ye. You or yer friend. This wound is serious."

His hand covered hers, emitting warmth and strength. Beads of sweat dotted his forehead. Even without her empathic skills, she knew he was barely holding onto consciousness. The boat's hull pounded beneath them.

"Bleeding hell," Alex shouted.

Roque's head snapped up.

Two vessels gave chase, the smaller lifting and falling with the waves. The slightly larger vessel gave the impression of a hag tottering on a cane in comparison. Smoke billowed from her aft as she fell quickly behind the other boat.

Alex furiously worked the strange mechanism, coaxing their little skiff to greater speed. Edeen's knees banged against the bottom. Grim faced, Alex searched the shoreline.

Edeen scanned the cliffs too. She knew this area. "Alex," she called out just as Roque slumped into her, as loose as though he were a hay-stuffed doll, pushing her over beneath his weight.

Alarmed, she slipped her hand onto his chest, waiting for the expansion of an exhalation, breathing with him when it finally came. The sea thumped beneath her bottom. She struggled to push Roque up enough that she could see over the side.

The smaller craft was gaining on them.

She'd lived her entire life on these wild cliffs and knew them as well as she knew her own heart. The water line was higher than she thought it should be though.

"Alex, over there."

She stretched her arm out wide to where a cleft cut into the foreboding cliffs where swollen rains ran off.

Alex's mouth formed a hard line.

"I know these seas!"

"But the landscape has changed—"

"Roque is unconscious. He needs help. Have you a better course?"

His knuckles squeezed around the steering stick, his arms tight, wrestling the roaring little monster.

"We cannot let that man near Roque."

As she shouted it, she knew the truth of those words. That *Geschopf* had hurt Roque before and would do so again. Anger gushed over her skin. "I've played among these cliffs since I was a child. I know a place those men will never find us."

Alex stared hard at her, his body strung tight like drying leather. Jaw clenched, he gave a brisk nod.

"Over there." Edeen pointed at a natural outbreak in the cliffs. "Take us close to that outcropping."

Though there was nothing but steep cliff walls and the surging slapping sea, Alex yanked the handle and the boat rose up on her side in a tight turn. Edeen slid with Rogue into the side.

"Closer," she yelled, her words snagged away by the buffeting of the waves and roar of the smoking monster. She searched for recognizable crags within the stone face. Cliff-nesting birds raged from their mud nests at their approach.

Alex brought them along the inside of the outcrop, out of sight of the other boats. For the moment.

"Here. 'Tis here."

He shut the little beast up and the boat slowed in the water. "There's nothing here," Alex hissed.

"Help me get him into the water." Edeen began pulling Rogue closer to the side.

Alex stumbled over, feet braced wide against a large

wave that crashed into the cliff walls and slapped back over them.

Edeen shook her wet hair out of her face. "There's a cavern right under our feet with a passage that leads to the top of the cliffs. Only a few from my village know of it."

He studied her sharply, obviously not liking it, but what choice did they have? With more strength than she had given his slim frame, Alex rolled Roque up and over the side. As the boat dipped, Edeen slid into the water with him, wrapping around the tall unconscious man, one arm hanging onto the side of the boat, grateful when Alex leaned over to pull Roque back up.

"You got him?"

"He's heavy," she admitted, gasping under the burden as water splashed into her face.

"Hold him a second." Alex let go and Edeen struggled to keep Roque's chin above water, more impossible with the rough choppy waves splashing over them. Alex's face popped back over the side. The lout was grinning. "Clear the boat." Unlooping his belt, he ran off toward the back.

Edeen shoved away from the side, kicking furiously to keep both herself and Roque afloat. Damned skirts fluffed up around them, but at least they were not tangling around their legs this time.

The smoking beast roared, spinning around and with a high-pitched shriek the boat sped back out toward open sea just as Alex dove off the back, a long bag on his shoulder.

A few broad strokes brought him to Edeen and immediately the majority of Roque's weight was taken from her.

"Hang onto us." She nodded, salt water slapping her face.

Alex laughed. "I'm pretty much committed now. Ready?"

Edeen smiled, liking his unflappable spirit. He reminded her of her younger brother, Col. "Aye."

With Roque between them, they took deep breaths and with a nod from Alex, they dove down. Noise and wind and slapping water against rock abruptly shut off.

They swam downward. Whatever was in Alex's bag was heavy, weighting them. Edeen hoped it wouldn't be too hard to pull up once she found the cavern.

It was dark. The sea water freezing and stinging her eyes. She guided them along the submerged cliff face, feeling for the familiar rounding and smoothing like the belly of a woman swollen with child, which meant the entrance was close.

Roque's legs and arms dragged. The water should have revived him. She could barely see. Though bunched together, the men's faces were little more than hazy orbs in the dark. Roque's longer dark hair floated in front of his face.

She gripped her fist tighter in Roque's shirt,

continuing to feel her way down the wall.

Here.

Relief burned through her lungs upon finding the small opening that would take them to an air-filled cavern. The need to take a breath was overpowering. A building pressure inside her ribs. They wouldn't be able to hold their breath much longer. And Roque? Unconscious, he had not been able to fill his lungs before they dragged him under.

Pausing only long enough to get Alex's attention, Edeen slipped into the narrow hole and grabbed Roque by the shoulders, pulling him in with her. There was not much space for them both, but that would only last a little while. She wished she had been able to warn Alex about how tight the tunnel was going to get and hoped he was not adverse to cramped dark spaces underwater.

Dragging Roque behind her, the rock closed in around them. She felt his larger frame snagging along the grainy ceiling. She could not see a blamed thing.

She pulled and pulled, the walls barreling in so tight she used her feet to push off them.

The walls opened, seeming to fall away abruptly. She pushed out into a world of air and the sound of splashing.

Heaving in a painful shallow gasp, Edeen hauled Roque up with her.

The dark was oppressively thick. Not just the dark of suddenly snuffed out candles, but a darkness that closed in, burying the world.

More splashing and the grating heave of Alex sucking in air. Then coughing.

Some of Rogue's weight was taken from her and the water pulsed against her legs as Alex treaded water for Roque. Several moments passed while they both dragged in air.

Roque's head lifted fractionally. Wet hair swiped across her cheek. Thank the gods, he was coming to.

"We need to get out of the water," Alex said. Before the cold numbed their hearts. A tremor rolled through her. So cold.

"There's a ledge." Her voice echoed around the cave walls. Water dripped on stone. "We can climb out. My brothers left torches and flint."

As long as she'd known this land, the water levels inside the cavern remained constant so even though the sea outside had risen, the ledge should be in the same place.

She tugged Roque toward where she judged the ledge to be.

Alex swam with her, taking the majority of Roque's weight.

"To your right," Roque rasped.

"Ah. You've rejoined us, then." Relief tempered the teasing tone of Alex's voice.

"Umn," Roque grunted. "Where in the blazes are we?"

Edeen's palm hit the ledge just where Roque had said it would be. How had he known?

"I'll hold him while you climb out, ma'am," Alex offered.

'Twas more difficult than expected to release Roque to another. What if Alex didn't have a good enough grip and they lost him to the darkness?

Which was a ridiculous thought. Alex was his friend. He'd not let him come to harm. He had already proven that.

She was glad the darkness hid her expression. She did not understand where this fervent protectiveness came from, or so quickly.

Pulling herself up onto the slippery shelf was harder than she remembered. Her arms shook and the gown kept getting in the way.

A sudden shove on her bottom propelled her onto her stomach on the ledge. A shocked gasp escaped her, again thankful for the concealing darkness. She did not ask which of the men had assisted her.

Scrambling the rest of the way out, she quickly turned on her knees to help Alex with Roque.

Reaching down, she accidentally struck a nose. Roque's, she thought. Dripping hands latched onto her wrists, guiding her hands down to slide onto soggy shoulders. By touch, she found his chest and slipped her arms beneath his armpits and around his back.

This close, his breath washed against her neck, warm on her wet skin. The muscles in his arms and back tighten as he pushed down on the ledge.

"Dammit, mate, go easy on the apple crumbles." With all the splashing, Alex must be helping from behind.

Edeen felt, more than heard, Roque's low chuckle. Alex grunted loud and Roque strained onto the ledge, or more precisely onto Edeen, though he quickly rolled off her with a muttered "sorry".

More splashing and grunting and the round part of a broad shoulder landed on her thigh, causing Edeen to hiss out in unexpected pain.

That shoulder also quickly rolled away.

"Ma'am. Sorry," Alex strained. "Many pardons. I'm so sorry."

"'Tis all right." She smothered a chuckle and stretched out her arms, half-sprawling on the slimy rock ledge, searching for the flint and torches Shaw and Col kept just out of the water's reach.

"What are you doing?" Roque asked. His voice sounded winded.

"Looking for the flint."

"Don't bother, Treasure."

Treasure? "Do not call me that. I'm no man's treasure."

"In that, you're sorely mistaken." A hint of laughter coated his voice.

39

There was a soft metallic ripping sound, the rustle of stiff material and a beam of light snicked on.

Edeen squinted at it. Strange magic.

Shivers ran through her. She stared at the small cylinder sprouting light that Alex had taken out of the now open bag he had brought from the boat. The bag's interior was shiny as though coated in oil to keep everything inside dry. And the objects within—an odd assortment of shiny objects similar to the longer sticks the men on top of the cliff had held. Some sort of club.

Alex poured the light over Roque. "Blimey, Roque, you look like shite."

Roque's lips tugged into a thin grin. Supporting himself with one arm, small tremors rolled through him. His face was pale, cheeks flushed with redness. Blood diluted pink with sea water soaked the side of his shirt.

Alex rummaged through the bag. "The bullet should have worked itself out by now. What's going on?" He pulled a small square box from the bag and clicked open a hinged lid.

"I don't know." A slow drop of water hovered at the top of a wet lock of hair before falling onto his cheek. "It feels different."

Alex's hand stilled in the process of lifting a square fold of linen from the box. His head snapped up, brows drawn tighter. "Different how?"

"Cold." Roque's arm gave out. He slipped before

catching himself.

Alex caught him by the shoulders at the same time Edeen got there.

Roque's head hung down. "I'm okay."

"Nay. Ye are not. Lie still against me." There wasn't much room on the ledge, but Edeen managed to get behind Roque and ease his shoulders and head back against her. It was a testament to how much pain he was in that she maneuvered him so complacently.

Bunching the wet shirt up, Alex pressed the cloth to the wound.

Roque hissed, stiffening. "Hey. Ow."

"Sorry, princess." Alex dabbed at the blood flow, trying to get a clear look at the round little wound. "So cold. And?"

The Adam's apple in Roque's throat column bounced. "I can feel it, but I can't push it out."

The men stared hard at each other, an unspoken conversation passing between them.

"Geschopf?" Alex growled. "New kind of weapon?"

"Designed especially for me."

"Dammit."

Edeen didn't understand everything they were talking about, but she had come to several conclusions on her own. First being, with Roque's ability to leap so far off that cliff, inhuman agility and enhanced vision in the dark, he was something beyond mortal.

Something, that in normal circumstances, could perform self-healing, except this Wulf Geschopf had pierced Roque with some sort of blade that his natural ability to mend was not able to repair.

Her hand strayed to her neck. 'Twas no longer bleeding, yet it stung a bit from the salt water. Vampire? Yet he'd been out in daylight. Nor did he seem like a vampire, even if she had ever met one, which she had not, but she just thought they would be . . . she didn't know. Different?

"Very well then." Alex unfolded a long thin length of linen from the box and began wrapping that around Roque's torso to keep the other now-bloodied square of cloth tight against Roque's side. "We need to get you some place where I can dig the bullet out."

"He needs a Healer Sorceress," Edeen insisted.

Alex yanked the knot tight on the linen. "I wouldn't let a *healer* within a foot of him." His tone bellowed like a hound protecting its master.

"Alex . . ." Roque warned. "It's all right."

Head lowered, the strain left Alex's shoulder. He shook his head and water drops fell from his close-cropped hair. His gaze sought Edeen's. "Ma'am, would you kindly show us the way out of here." He held the short staff of light out to her.

"Of course." She took it, smoothing her thumb along the strange and wonderful device. Surely a powerful

42

sorcerer must have conjured it, trapping an eternal flame behind the round piece of glass. She pointed the end around the wet cavern, amazed at how the light beam cut so precisely through the darkness.

She set the beam back onto the men, brows rising at the amused expressions and quickly angled the light toward the way out.

There were three holes. The center one looked as though 'twas the most reliable to take as the hole was as tall and wide as a large man and on the same level as the ledge. Yet she knew from childhood exploration that 'twas the most treacherous path with unforeseen drop-offs with no end. Or at least too deep to hear any of the stones they'd dropped into it hit bottom.

The tunnel to the left came to a dead stop several twists in, yet there was a small unassuming slant of a hole higher up on the right, that once one climbed into, opened to a sloping tunnel that led to the sheep-grazing meadow at the top of the sea cliffs.

She set the light device down inside the hole just above her shoulder and went back to Alex and Roque.

"We need to get him up inside there. Do ye think he can manage?"

"You realize I'm right here and can speak for myself," Roque muttered. "I can get in there."

He pulled himself straight and immediately sagged back.

43

Soft shivers rolled through Edeen, her skin puckering from the cold air and dampness of her wet dress. Glancing at each other, she and Alex each took one of Roque's arms and hauled him to his feet.

"You all right?" Alex asked.

Roque nodded, mouth tight, and held a tight palm against his side.

Edeen remained quiet, recognizing the frustration for what it was. She had three brothers, and not one handled being laid low by illness or injury well.

The overgrown infants.

And if Roque was accustomed to healing quickly, facing any weakness 'twould be new and doubly frustrating for him.

Alex squinted up into the tight hole. "This is good. Even if Geschopf or any of his men found the underwater entrance I doubt they'd pick this slash as the tunnel to follow."

Roque stepped up onto a boulder and braced his arms to pull himself up. "Don't underestimate the man. Has the nose of a damned bloodhound."

"But surely the water—" Alex started.

Roque turned back, his face stern. "Do not underestimate him."

Alex swallowed . . . and nodded before locking his hands together to give Roque a higher boost up.

Setting his foot in Alex's hands, he braced shaking

arms on the lip of the hole, and Roque scrambled up inside and disappeared from view.

There were some scraping noises and the light source lifted to the ceiling, withdrew, then angled outward so Edeen and Alex could better see.

"All right, luv, come on up."

Before she could even respond, Alex took her around the waist and lifted. Damn skirts got in the way again, the wet fabric pooling under her knees as she landed. She had to release the folds to crawl out of the way, moving just as Alex tossed the bag up, took a running leap and scrambled up.

Bunching up the filthy sagging skirts around her thighs, Edeen crawled to the point where the tunnel opened up in height, though there was room only to walk two men abreast.

Roque was on his feet, though barely. Leaning against the wall, head hanging so low his chin touched the top of his chest.

Standing and dropping her skirts, Edeen went to him, tucking herself beneath his arm. She didn't like the low tremors that ran through him or the terrible heat emanating off his skin, which was strange since she herself was freezing. She pushed in closer against him, reveling in his warmth, even as she hoped to cool his fever down with the coldness of her body. His chest was firm and wide, stomach tight, and his heavy arm felt nice around her.

'Twas pragmatism, she told herself. He needed cooling and she needed warmth. And if she happened to enjoy being so close to him, what harm was there in that?

"Come away, 'tis not far." Squeezed beneath his arm, their shoulders both bumped into the earthen walls on each side, even as Roque leaned farther in against her.

Alex walked closely behind them, bringing the bag. "Let me take him." He was practically on top of her, ready to catch Roque up should he suddenly give out.

"In a moment." The aid would be appreciated, even though she was loathe to give up his warmth. Each faltered step, Roque leaned more heavily into her. She was barely managing beneath his weight as 'twas. "A few more steps and the tunnel widens. The way out is not far beyond that."

She stepped on the bottom of her dragging gown and stumbled, jarring her shoulder into the wall.

Alex caught her from behind, while Roque shifted his weight away from her.

"Ma'am?" Alex kept her steady.

"I'm fine. The water's dragging these skirts down."

"You need use of your hands to hold up your dress," Roque said. "I've got if from here."

Pushing off the wall, he began walking.

Edeen frowned at his retreating back. "He's a bit of stubbornness to him, has he not?"

A grin coated Alex's voice. "You have no idea."

They followed Roque, the beam from Alex's curious little light bounced along the uneven walls as he walked.

The tunnel widened enough for the three of them to walk apace. Without asking, Edeen and Alex immediately flanked Roque, each slinging one of his arms over their own shoulders.

Apparently none too soon as he sank against them, his steps more dragging than supporting his own weight.

Heat poured off him. When the light passed across him from Alex's gait, Edeen could see fissures of steam lifting off Roque's wet clothes. The wet ends of his dark hair curled at the nape of his neck.

Once again, she sifted through her essence, trying to find the missing source of her empathic abilities and get a hint of what Roque truly was, yet there was nothing there. The absence of her gift frightened her. She'd rather have lost the ability to walk.

"Please tell me that's not your way out," Alex said.

Edeen lifted her head and the world nipped out of her grasp. Alex played the light over the space where their exit hole should be, but 'twas no longer there.

The space where the opening should be was obvious, but it had been sealed off by stone and mortar.

They were trapped.

Chapter Five

This wasn't right. Why would anyone build a wall across the entrance?

And so quickly.

Shaw had stashed a bunch of supplies here, in case things went bad with the witch, only two days ago when their small group left on the foray to search out Aldreth's castle for weaknesses and rescue Toren.

The supplies that were now gone.

"I do not understand. How is a wall here?" She demanded as though Roque and Alex had anything to do with it.

Propping Roque against the earthen tunnel wall, Alex squinted at her. Roque looked done in. His slight glance toward her revealed glassy eyes as Alex helped him slide down the wall to sit.

Edeen sank down beside them, worry knotting her insides. She had led them here to this trap when Roque desperately needed a Healer Sorceress.

Could this be Aldreth's doing? If the witch knew about their clan's hidden stashes, she would be keen to cut them off from it.

Yet this had been such a small cache, hardly worth the effort. Also, Edeen felt no trace of magic humming across it, like the magical barrier that surrounded Aldreth's castle.

Of course, Edeen could not rely on her senses to ferret out magic at the moment.

But . . . her empathic ability aside, her instincts were wailing.

Everything was too strange, somehow off. The noisy magical boat, the men's strange manner of dress and speech. Both Englishmen, yet she couldn't make sense of some of their words.

Her heart clenched in her chest.

The last memory before waking in the smugglers cave was of Aldreth hurting Toren while she heedlessly ran to stop the witch. Everything after that was gone.

Oh, Toren, what have ye done? As a sorcerer, he could send her through a rift in time. But why? If indeed 'twas what happened. Why would they not have taken her to *Reolin Skene* and the Shadowrood?

They would have if they had been able.

Her heart wrung tighter.

Sweet peace, what happened to her brothers?

"We have two choices," Alex said, opening the bag.

Roque's lashes lifted, the only indication he was still with them and listening.

"Go back the way we came to the sea. Of course, we no longer have a boat and Geschopf is most probably still skulking about."

Roque grunted.

"Or get that bloody bullet out of you right here."

Roque lifted his hand weakly. "*That* I'm in favor of."

Alex smiled.

The situation couldn't be much worse. They had enemies behind them, a wall to the front and a man spilling his life's blood that he could not afford to lose.

She should not have brought them here. "Forgive me."

Roque took her hand within his warm grasp and squeezed. Emotions rolled through her, vague and indescript, yet there like a forgotten dream lying just at the edge of remembering. Her gift. Edeen gasped and her essence wavered. She tried to clasp onto it, yet the feeling floated away as wispy as mist through her fingers.

Roque stared uncertainly at her.

"This is going to hurt." Alex produced a short blade that folded out from a smooth iron hilt of the same size. *A small hidden folding blade. Ingenious.*

They needed to get Roque out of here. Get him help, but that wasn't possible. Alex seemed to know what he was doing.

Edeen shifted on her knees. "How can I help?"

"Hold this." Alex slapped the light rod into her hands. "I need to get the bullet out."

"Bullet?" She tried the foreign word. Had the tip of a blade broken inside of Roque? The term was unfamiliar.

This was definitely not her time. Toren must have sent her through time.

Wild panic began swelling in her chest, the truth daggered and brutally sharp.

Roque's soft grunt wrenched her back to him. He curled over his wound, his hand pawing the loose soil beneath him.

Alex had one palm flat on Roque's stomach, the other held the small knife, rooting around in the wound. "Hold still."

Edeen held the light steady, choking down the nausea welling up along with Roque's blood. She grasped Roque's hand, stopping him from digging. He latched on to her with an intensity that was jarring and ground his head back against the wall. The tendons in his neck bulged. His eyes squeezed shut.

"Breathe through it," she coaxed.

"Hurry it up, dammit. I can—feel. It," Roque panted. "It's burrowing deeper."

Alex's head snapped up, lines of worry creasing his forehead. His troubled gaze sought Edeen before lowering his eyes back to his task. "Just hang on. I've got this."

Jaw clenched, Roque nodded, putting all his trust in his friend and Edeen's heart went out to these two men.

Beads of perspiration broke out across Alex's brow. A muscle in his cheek jumped every time Roque flinched, though his hands remained steady.

And Roque...low tremors rolled through his body. Steam lifted from his hot flesh as though fire burned from within. His head rocked side-to-side along the wall, yet he remained as still as he could bear. The amount of endurance and trust Roque showed was stunning.

His breathing grew shallow, ragged. Edeen squeezed his hand in an attempt to anchor him. She wished Charity was here.

"Got it," Alex gritted out. "Elusive little bugger." He twisted the blade, blood-coated fingers up to the last knuckles within the wound.

Roque sucked in a breath between his teeth, every muscle stiff as a plank.

He screamed as Alex pulled a hissing glowing oblong bit of bloodied metal from his flesh and immediately went limb, losing his hold on consciousness.

"Whoa, whoa." Alex tried to steady Roque without letting the *bullet* touch his skin.

"I have him." Edeen drew Roque's head and shoulders into her lap. "What is that?" She gestured toward the small piece of iron Alex pulled from Roque's side.

"The bullet?" He frowned at it for a moment before putting in a pocket sewn into the sides of his breeches. "It's trouble."

He glanced about the cave. "I need something to stop the bleeding."

"Here." Edeen eased Roque's head from her lap and got to her feet. She reached behind her back to loosen the cross ties of her gown. 'Twas wet and cumbersome anyway, though if her brothers caught her traipsing about in only her underskirts, well, that couldn't be helped at the moment. She shimmied out of it and let the heavy material drop to the ground. Shivers prickled her skin through the lighter fabric of her chemise. "Give me the knife."

"Your skirts?" Alex held the knife to her hilt first, his gaze averted to her feet, one bared. She'd lost both slippers and a stocking in the sea.

She looked down at herself, at the way the thin wet material clung to her, revealing her skin beneath. Her brothers would be furious with her, which brought a touch of warmth to her chest, imaging their ire, knowing it would never last as far as she was concerned. She took the blade and began cutting into the gown, ripping out a strip that she immediately pressed to Roque's wound. His head rolled to the side and his features screwed up in pain.

Alex took the knife and began cutting the bottom of her gown into more strips.

"Ye were going to tell me of this *bull-et*."

"I was?" Alex's tone was as flat as an anvil's head.

Edeen arched a brow, tired of evasive answers.

Alex's lips pulled down and he nodded, seeming to come to a decision. Twisting, he grabbed something out of his long bag and held it out for her to see. "Okay, then.

Modern weaponry in a jiff. This is a gun."

Edeen nodded at the odd shaped black metal. It had an obvious handle and a short hollow shaft. Alex yanked a thin box out from the handle and took a pointed oval silver piece from within and held it up to her. "This is a bullet. One of these was shot into Roque."

"From this *gun*." She ran a finger along the gun's stock, imagining how the little silver bullet fit perfectly within the hollowed inside. "Shot like an arrow?"

The corner of Alex's lip lifted. "Similar. No strings, but a small explosion in this chamber here, propels the bullet forward."

Edeen nodded, getting the concept, but not liking it. 'Twould require little skill or strength to use these weapons. "Those men on the cliffs, they used these guns upon us."

"Yes."

"Theirs were longer."

Again, Alex nodded. "Rifles."

"*Ri-fuls*," Edeen tested the new word, her stomach queasy. "This *bull-et* that found Roque . . . 'tis different."

Alex's eyes went hard. He lifted the little piece of metal like it offended him. "Engineered especially to take Roque down."

She withdrew the fabric to inspect Roque's wound. The bleeding had lessened quite a bit. In fact the skin around the edges already seemed less rough, as though they were smoothing together. She'd witnessed ruined flesh knit together a few times before, but only under the hands of a Healer Sorceress.

"What is Roque?"

Alex looked away, troubled. He wiped the blood from his hands.

"I know he's more than human," she added. A muscle twitched in Alex's cheek at his slight half-grin. "You figured that out on your own?"

"Alex."

The grin slid away as though it never existed. "That's Roque's place to tell."

She was about to argue that point when Alex curled his hand and grimaced, The tips of his fingers were white as though burned, before the point of blistering. She grabbed his hand. "What's happened?"

He tried to pull back. "Nothing."

"Ye've burned them." She scowled. "The *bull-et*?"

Her breath hitched when he wouldn't answer. She looked down at the sweat dotting Roque's skin. She'd thought the heat pouring off him was fever. "His blood burns?"

"No, it's not hot enough, but—"

"Deep inside, he boils." Edeen mulled that over. "And ye knew that."

Alex shrugged and pulled his hand from hers. "He needed that *bullet* out." Taking a small flat flask from the bag, Alex poured what looked like water over his hand.

A lump formed in her throat. "Here, let me see." Edeen took one of the smaller strips he'd made from her gown.

"I've got it." He grabbed the fabric out of her hand. "I'm medically trained. I can handle it." Ah, male pride she was all too familiar with.

She nodded, and folded another piece of her gown into a square, which she placed against Roque's wound, holding it there while she used another length to wrap around his torso to keep it in place. Roque's brows pulled together in sleep. Undergoing a healing from a Healer Sorceress was sometimes more of an ordeal than the original hurt. She wondered if whatever was happening inside Roque's body was equally as painful. She glanced sidewise at Alex, who was wrapping his burned hands, wiggling his fingers to make sure he hadn't gotten the makeshift bandages too tight. "Tell me who these people after us are. Please, Alex. That man—he has hurt Roque before, hasn't he?"

He didn't answer for a while. He tied off his knot and then picked up the *gun*, all traces of softness gone. He replaced the bullet and clicked the little box back into the handle. Instead of returning it to the bag, he slipped the gun into the waist at the back of his breeches.

He wasn't going to tell her and Edeen suspected she knew why.

"I know this is no longer my time."

Alex's gaze locked on her face, stunned.

She gave him a brave smile, though his expression confirmed her fears. She tied a knot in Roque's bandage, hoping Alex didn't notice how bad her hands were shaking.

Alex nodded. "We're at war."

"The Chieftains?"

He smiled kindly and shook his head. "It's larger than that. Many countries are involved."

She nodded for him to go on.

"Scotland and England are allies."

"Allied with you English?"

"Turns out we have a greater common enemy."

"The men on the cliff."

"Nazis. They seek to subjugate all of Europe beneath their rule."

Edeen sensed there was much much more to it that Alex wasn't going into. Anger poured off of him. She flicked her senses out, seeking some semblance of her lost gift. "That man who leaped from the cliff. He is a Nazi?"

Alex's lips went light. "The worst kind. He's a leader in the *Schutzstaffel*, the SS—Hitler's personal police force." He stopped himself, searching for words familiar to her. "The Nazi leader's personal guard. His task is to gather those of rare supernatural ability to use—"

"As weapons," she finished. This Hitler's goal was not far different from what Aldreth intended. The witch sought to use Toren, and by extension their entire clan through him, to increase her magical strength.

"This Geschopf is after Roque."

"He's been after Roque a long time."

Because Roque's magical talent is rare.

"He captured him before," Alex's voice sounded like soft steps walking on gravel. "Did terrible things. Roque won't speak of it."

A fierce protectiveness surged inside Edeen's bosom. "Yet he exposed himself to the *Nazis* to come after me."

"He was the only one who could."

Edeen swept her hand up to the puncture wounds at her neck.

"We couldn't allow an empath as powerful as yourself to get into *Nazi* hands."

"I understand." She did. Shaw had been willing to take their entire clan to the Shadowrood to keep their magic from being tainted by the witch, and thereafter tainting the world. An ache shimmered behind her eyes at knowing Roque thought of her as little more than a weapon to be kept from this Hitler and how he'd laughed when she'd told him she no longer felt her gift. And if it came back? What would he do with her then?

It wouldn't matter. She'd seek out a sorcerer to send her back to her own time where she belonged.

"I understand what this Hitler wants of me, but what of you? What do you and Roque expect of me?"

Alex looked away. His Adam's apple jumped in his throat, and then nodding to himself as though he came to a decision, his gaze cut back to her. "We're not as sinister as that, I promise you." His lips twisted downward. "I work with military intelligence. That means nothing to you." He shook his head. "It's my job to intercept messages being relayed between our enemies."

"So you capture couriers?"

He smiled. "Not exactly. We have machines that are able to transmit messages through the air."

Edeen's eyes widened.

Alex winced at her expression, but went on, probably realizing most of what he said wouldn't make sense anyway. "We can pluck the messages out of the air, but the Germans know this so they have encoded them."

He waited for her nod to continue. "They change the codes so frequently, they invented a machine to decipher them. It's called an enigma and unknown to the *Nazis*, we've captured one from their subs, er, another type of ship," he added. Pride poured off of him. The taking of this enigma must have been a great feat.

"I don't understand what that has to do with me."

"Well, so far, we haven't been able to crack the code. We will, but it's taking time."

"And time means more warriors lost. I do not have

any use with codes, or with *machines*. These things are all strange to me, you must realize this."

"We do, but that's not it." His lips firmed. "We did capture a courier. From the sub. He knows the codes."

"But will not speak." Her voice went flat. "For something of such import, surely your people have tried other methods."

Alex didn't blink at the accusation. "Even when he breaks, the codes are changed so rapidly, even he won't remember them all."

She exhaled, understanding dawning. "Yet an empath could search his memories and find every last code."

Alex nodded.

Edeen shook her head and Roque shifted in his sleep. "But they would be old codes."

"With enough of them, we would learn basic patterns and be able to decipher the new codes as they come through. Look, I know this is a lot to take in and so quickly, but it is important."

Her hand strayed to the little puncture wounds on her neck, her mind reeling. She had been hurled into another century's war. She didn't know how she had gotten here or why? Or how Alex and Roque knew to come to the cliffs to find an empath in the first place. A sudden thought occurred to her. What if a sorcerer from this time had plucked her from her family for this exact purpose? If so, she needed to find him and make him send her back. If searching a courier's memories was the price to find this sorcerer, she would gladly do it. That is, if she could summon her gift at all.

Edeen nodded. She didn't know what she was dealing with and didn't want to seem too eager to help. "I'll think on it, Alex. Right now, 'tis all so much."

"I understand." He seemed so genuine, she wanted to trust him.

"What do we do now?"

"Wait. Get some rest and allow Roque time to heal."

Now that the rare *bull*-et was gone from his body, Alex seemed certain Roque could mend on his own.

Edeen ran the back of her hand across Roque's forehead, pushing his wet hair back in the process. He was still warm to the touch.

"And what then?" she asked. "We are still trapped."

Alex smiled at that, his eyes sparking with the trace of a secret.

"Go to sleep." He stretched out on the ground, using his bag to pillow his head. "It's not as hopeless as it seems."

Chapter Six

Fire coiled beneath his blood, raw, savage, an inferno. At fourteen, his first transformation should not be upon him for months yet.

"Give him more." Geschopf shouted, the vein at his forehead bulging purple behind his skin. "See what he can take."

Liquid ice poured through his veins from the needle violating the inside of his elbow. He screamed, a raw, guttural sound born of violation. He clenched down on a swell of fire. He would not transform. He would not. Geschopf wanted him to, wanted more than anything for Roque to become a dragon, and Roque knew deep down that if he did, if he gave into it under the Black Claw's ministrations, he would be lost. Geschopf would own his soul.

Roque lurched out of sleep, gasping, flames sprouting off his skin, catching on his clothes.

"Peace, ye're well." The woman, Edeen crooned, holding his shoulder down over the part of his shirt that did not burn. Coming to himself, he quickly quenched the fire within, patting the flames out on his arms and chest.

"Ye dreamed." Edeen watched him warily.

Roque looked away and swallowed, recoiling from the

images lingering behind his eyes. *Geschopf. Experiments. Cages. Pain. So much pain. He hadn't transformed. He never transformed.* His heart pulsed erratically. He had not dreamed of his youth in a long time.

He searched the darkness, his draconic senses stroking along the rich minerals embedded in the stone, thrusting into a multitude of veins and tunnels. He felt the cliffs, old and heavy around them. He sensed the caverns below the waves, a bullet he could not push out, a woman's heartbeat pushing sweet blood through a lush body tied to the magic of the earth stronger than any the dragon had detected before. Old magic, like his own.

His side still throbbed. He looked down to inspect his wound, but found silky fabric wrapped around his torso, moist and steaming from the heat of his skin. She had given up her dress to make bandages for him.

He lifted his gaze and was struck by the flawlessness of the woman. She had stripped down to her undergarments. The thin white chemise was still damp on her form, pulled tight around her curves and satin skin. His mouth suddenly went dry.

Treasure. The dragon scraped to the surface for a closer look. "Are you all right?"

Startled green eyes widened. "I'm well."

He tilted his head, studying. It surprised her that he'd asked how she fared. Considering she had awoken into a new world scant hours before, snagged off a cliff and shot at, she was handling things remarkably well.

His gaze drifted to the wounds at her neck—his bite—and heat flared in his blood. *Possessive*.

What was he going to do with her? His job was to keep her from *Nazi* hands, but handing her over to the Allied Command didn't sit well with him either. Even if she could help with the enigma machine and gods knows what else, it wasn't right to use her.

"Has your gift returned?"

Long lashes lowered, splaying like bruises upon pale cheeks. "Nay," she whispered, her tone betraying loss. It was like listening to heartbreak. He felt like a cad for being relieved, yet without her empathic abilities, Allied Command would have no use for her.

Hitler would have no use for her.

She would be safe.

Despair splashed over his heart. That was a hopeless wish. There was no safety for her. Even without her gift, there would always be those who disbelieved. She'd forever be hunted.

A protectiveness seared Roque's heart, a raging inferno.

"Why is that man after you?"

Direct. Roque appreciated that. He glanced at Alex slumbering on his side, quietly snoring. "Alex didn't explain?"

"He said it was not his place." She carded her palms

64

together, placing them primly in her lap. "So I am asking you." She gave him the look of a woman expecting to get her way. Which sent a tingly fissure of delight into his belly.

She frowned when he didn't immediately answer. "I know I've come through time."

Slept through it more precisely. "Alex told you that?"

She nodded and a waft of sea water drifted from her wild tousled hair. He wanted to reach out and feel it between his fingers.

"What else did he tell you?"

"That ye're at war. That this Hitlam—"

"Hitler."

"Hitler seeks to use my gifts as a weapon." Her tone sharpened with disgust. "Roque, does he also seek you as a weapon?"

The concern in her eyes speared straight to his gut, unraveling the hard wall he'd spent years in building. The dragon moved, scales rubbing across scales rumbled in his ears.

Her hand slipped to the puncture wounds at her neck. "Ye're of the race of vampires."

She'd put it all together. Roque stiffened. She would know vampires were born of magic that was dark, yet her features held no disgust. Or fear . . . and the hard shell coating Roque's emotions cracked a little bit more. He very nearly told her about being a dragon as well.

"Yet ye're also different than most vampires." Her brows creased. "Why did ye bite me?"

Again, shock splintered his system. Vampire. To most people blood addiction was the only association they had with vampires. Monstrous, vile addicts that sucked people dry. Monsters. Yet here Edeen sat, not even considering that he had bitten her for his own personal high.

His heart swelled at the wonderment of her.

Dark lashes swept up, revealing intense green eyes and he realized she waited for an answer.

"To wake you."

Her eyes narrowed, head tilted in a gesture of *go on*.

This wouldn't be easy for her to hear, not with her brother's part in it. "You didn't travel to this century through a sorcerer's rift."

"Then how—?"

"You slept."

"Slept." A wisp of an incredulous smile lifted a corner of her lip. "For a hundred years. 'Tis impossible."

"Close to seven centuries." His tone held the same weight as a grave marker.

Edeen's shoulders stiffened. "Ye're serious?"

Roque shifted up, ignoring the bracing ache in his side. Alex mumbled in his sleep. The man was a brilliant strategist, but could sleep through machine gun fire. He'd seen it.

Edeen rocked forward, her arms pressed tight against

her stomach. "How? How is that possible?"

Roque leaned forward as well, so that his forehead almost touched hers. He spoke quietly to not awaken Alex. "We don't know exactly how it was done. That kind of magic hasn't been known for generations. Not since—"

Her head snapped up, nearly colliding with his nose. "Tell me."

"From what we could piece together—mostly from legend and oral history that was finally written centuries later. . . ." Questionable at best. "There was a battle on Crunfathy Hill between your brothers and a witch."

"Aye." Edeen's heart rate was slowing. "Aldreth."

He took her hand. It was cold. "The histories didn't say."

Edeen's hand trembled. "She meant to force Toren, my brother a powerful sorcerer, to give her all his magic by blending with her and by extension the magic of our clan." Her eyes swept up. "All magic would have darkened."

He failed. Magic is darkness, he didn't tell her. Instead he said, "In the battle on the hill, something happened. You were hurt, put into a deep slumber that even your sorcerer brother could not undo."

"The smugglers cave?" Now her pulse sped up. He could sense the blood pumping wildly through her thin veins. "He took me to the smugglers cave."

"I'm sorry."

She didn't respond. Silence thrummed through the

stale chilly air of the cave. Alex roused, shifting his head on the ruck sack. His neck would have a fine crick, but Roque wasn't inclined to wake him just yet. His gaze tracked onto the bandages wrapped around Alex's hands, at the redness of his skin and a jolt shot through him. *Dammit, Alex.* He knew exactly what had happened. Guilt thudded into his gut like a gavel.

"Your brother must have loved you very much."

"Why do you say that?"

So much loss and vulnerability spilled through her tone, Roque's heart shattered for her.

"He wouldn't let you die." Nor would he, he vowed, not knowing where the sudden sentiment came from. "Toren couldn't wake you, yet he made certain you'd be safe, hidden, preserved within spells upon spells. It must have taken every ounce of his strength to achieve that."

Edeen nodded, never doubting her brother's devotion and Roque suddenly longed to know what that felt like, that surety of love.

Alex stirred again and they went quiet. "Is it breakfast yet?" Alex drawled, one eye cracking open and stretched his arms. Roque wondered how long he'd been awake and listening. "Cor, my neck hurts."

Chapter Seven

There was no way around it. Roque had to use dragon fire to get through the bricks. Now that Geschopf's bullet was out, he had the strength to do it, but . . . he glanced at Edeen.

Her features were scrunched, watching him intently, uncertain of what he was up to.

She was about to get an eyeful.

She accepted him being a vampire easily enough, which brought a new surge of tenderness just thinking of that, yet a dragon?

There wasn't much hope for it. Besides she had already witnessed fire drift off his skin, though she had not brought it up.

He turned back to the bricks, gathering the fire to his belly, building. A tight vibration pressed against his head. The dragon roused within him. Bringing fire from his core was always a risk, especially when he tried to focus the generated heat in large bursts. Drawing so much fire forth all at once came dangerously close to letting the dragon free and he could never do that. Never transform. He learned that much from Geschopf, though it was not the lesson *Die Schwarzen Klaue* had meant to teach. Once transformed, he would become an untamed creature of nature, feral, acting from primeval instinct. Something Geschopf could shape and mold to his liking. He would no longer be himself. That was his greatest fear.

Carefully, he soothed the beast within, treading lightly around his core and fanned the flames, allowing the fire to pool inside his veins where he let it burst forth, erupting through his fingertips.

He shot a steady stream of fire into a line of mortar between the bricks.

Edeen gasped. He felt her shift back, felt the rhythm of her heart speed up. Alex's pulse, also, picked up. Even with all they'd been through together, Roque rarely exposed so much of his fire.

Roque didn't look back, a little hesitant of what he'd find in their expressions, so he poured his focus into his flame, drilling through the mortar with the precision of a light machine gun.

He moved from one line of mortar to another below that until, with nothing to hold them, the bricks fell upon themselves.

Extinguishing his flame, Roque still did not look back. Mortar dust and debris floated in the dark air.

Edeen's blood pumped crazily, a fluttering punch to his gut.

He flinched when she moved to his side.

"By the rood, vampires have changed these past centuries." Wonder filled the lush tones of her voice.

Alex chuffed out a laugh.

Roque's gaze snapped to Edeen's profile and something alien and tender curled around his chest. She looked at the broken bricks with something akin to awe.

Alex pushed the ruck sack between them, shoving past as he bent and stepped over the pile of bricks. "Shall we, then?" The handle of his Enfield revolver gleamed from the back of his waistband.

Glancing at each other, Edeen and Roque followed suit. They passed into some sort of storeroom basement. Large marked bags and boxes on shelves lined the walls, with more bins and smaller boxes atop wooden tables in the center of the room. One wall was made with shelving for wine and casks, though most the places were empty, the distinct indicator of wartime rationing.

Edeen stared wide-eyed at the assortment of goods.

Roque moved toward the stairs, motioning for Edeen and Alex to stay behind him. His keen sense of hearing picked up movement upstairs, lots of talking. Lots of heartbeats.

He waited at the top of the steps, listening at the door. Simple idle chatter. Edeen and Alex moved up behind him.

He cracked open the door and a riot of sounds and smells wafted over him. Spices, leather, paper. When he pushed the door open farther, all conversation halted.

Seven faces, waiting in queue at a small country store, ration books in hand, turned toward them

71

"Hey now," the store clerk lifted her stamp. "What're ye doing down there?"

Roque gave her a dazzling smile and she instantly cut off, her round face reddening. "There's a hole in your cellar. Did you know that, luv?"

Her brows rose into her hairline. He had them all truly well and flustered. Edeen and Alex scurried past him toward the opposite door.

"You should plug that up again if you ask me, now shouldn't you." He smiled and rushed out the door into a bright afternoon. Roque lifted his face to the sunlight, the dragon within preening, absorbing the warming rays.

Beside him, he detected a small intake of breath from Edeen, the smallest fissure of wariness.

"'Tis no longer a meadow." Her hand found his and Roque was inordinately pleased that she'd sought him for even a small reassurance.

He squeezed her fingers. Her gaze tracked around the whitewashed houses and black electrical lines that crossed above the hard-packed dirt street. A woman walked by and Edeen's eyes went wide at the short tight skirt and nylons with the black seam running down the back, the rolled back hair. A lorry passed by, lifting a cloud of dirt and smelling of petrol, and her heart rate fluttered.

By all accounts this was a small seaside village, but all the modernizations must be miracle overload to her. She was taking it in remarkably well and a tendril of pride burrowed its way closer to his heart. Edeen was getting to him more than anyone had in a long long time—probably ever if he was truthful with himself.

Roque let his arm slip around her waist, offering what small comfort he dared without falling until she leaned in closer. Such a miniscule action shouldn't have the power to drop him over the edge, but there he was, breath stilling and sailing through the air.

"We need transportation," he said to Alex, more to ground himself.

"Back," Alex hissed, grabbing the back of their clothes and pulling them both back into the shadows of the store front.

Not questioning Alex's order, they ducked behind a tall pile of cut peat at the side of the building. Alex angled his head to the right. "Two SS guys loitering over by the Tailor Shop." Though they were in plain-clothes, they still stood out.

Are they . . . ?" Alex's mouth twisted. "Is that a *krampus*?"

Sure enough, at least one of the SS soldiers bore the leathery smashed-up goat-ish features and wild coarse black hair. His cap undoubtedly concealed angled horns.

Damn, Geschopf most likely had men stationed about the small village and along the country roadways, counting on the fact that if Roque and Edeen survived the sea, they'd have to come to the village for either a radio or transportation.

"Wait here." Roque shifted to go take care of them.

Alex latched onto his arm. "Hey. Your I'm-a-big-bad-indestructible-vampire approach won't work this time."

Roque grinned. "It always works."

"Not while they're sporting those new bullets, it won't."

Roque stopped and rubbed a hand across his jaw. "Right, then. That is a bit of a disappointment, isn't it?"

Alex huffed, shaking his head.

"A less conspicuous getaway it is." Roque took Edeen's hand again. "Stay low."

They edged back along the wall and behind the store, onto a dirt path that ran between two white-washed fishermen cottages—turned *Talson Inn* by the hanging sign with *Tail O the Fox Pub* taking up the shorter adjacent cottage. A man and woman crossed the street and went into the inn.

Sitting around the corner was an old battered Ford, ripe for the picking.

"Think you can get that started?"

Alex threw him his patented do-you-need-to-ask glare and they scurried out into the road just as two more Germans rounded the side of the inn.

Eyes widening, both SS men went for their concealed guns.

Chapter Eight

An old man stepped out of the pub, tipping his hat when he saw them.

"Good day," Roque practically shoved Edeen through the open doorway while latching onto Alex's rucksack and dragging the younger man with them and found himself staring into the faces of half a dozen ghouls, mostly old sea-faring ghouls that carried the tales of a hard life etched into the crevices of their leather-gray faces. The ghouls gave them a steady look over.

Pipe smoke coated the air, heavy and rich of Cavendish tobacco, displacing the underlying smell of rotted flesh. Roque winced, eyeing the serving platters around the room, knowing ghouls' propensity for graveyards and *aged* meat. Sometimes preternatural senses weren't all that desirable. It stank to the point of nausea. Time to go. Roque scanned the room, searching for an exit point, not willing to engage if any of the old gents had that in mind.

Edeen, on the other hand, didn't have the same qualms and exclaimed, "There's men coming in here to abduct us. *Sassenachs*."

Every craggy head swiveled to her, taking in her ragged underskirts and disheveled appearance, and seemingly as one, the ghouls rose, roaring their indignation. Leave it to the romantic heart of a Scottish ghoul to rise to the defense of a maiden without question.

Edeen smiled up at him, smugly proud of herself.

Alex tsked behind him. "There'll be no livin with her now."

The two Germans burst into the room.

"It's them," Alex took up Edeen's ploy. So help him, if he cried "save us" Roque was going to swat him. Instead Alex pointed. "Those men. One's a *krampus. Nazis*," he added for emphasis and had to duck out of the way as one of the ghouls leapt over a table.

Roque winced, spotting a cane swinging toward the two fellows who were abruptly surrounded by an angry, gnashing mob. He almost felt sorry for them. Almost.

A chair skittered across the floor.

"Out the back, dearies." The grizzled barkeep, cricket paddle in fist, beckoned them to follow.

Roque dodged a flying spittoon, yanking Edeen out of the path of a rolling table.

Alex grabbed a half-drunk pint of ale and gulped it down as he flew after them.

The barkeep pulled open a door in the back and led them through a small apartment. "Ye'll have tae take the window."

Roque clasped his hand. "Our gratitude."

"Aye." The ghoul lifted the paddle in a mock salute.

"Tae hell with Hitler." Grinning broadly, he dashed back out the way he came.

"God love a riled Scotsman." Alex shoved open the window and rolled outside.

"Right. Out we go, Treasure." Without asking her permission, Roque swept Edeen up, cumbersome skirts and all, and carried her through the window, scraping his back in the tight fit.

"Stop calling me that," she railed.

He hit the ground on the run, not letting Edeen down, not until he had her tucked away somewhere safe.

Several children played ball in the back alley, human and ghoul.

Alex had already climbed into a rusty old lorry, hunched over to get at the wiring beneath the dashboard.

"Halt!"

Roque froze.

"It's him," Edeen whispered, able to see over his shoulder, though Roque already knew who it was. Wulf Geschopf's voice plagued every wretched broken strand left of his soul.

The children stopped. The ball rolled across the ground, bouncing into the upturned heel of Geschopf's boot.

Edeen pulled out of Roque's arms and immediately shouted at the children, shooing them away. "Run! Invaders are upon us. Run!"

Invaders?

"*Nazis*," Roque snarled, showing his pointed incisors and flung out his arms and the children screamed, scattering.

Geschopf bellowed. The ghouls and villagers slammed out of doorways, mothers screaming for their children.

Geschopf lifted his luger at Roque . . . and the old lorry screeched to a stop between them, heavy grey petrol fumes, clouding out of the gurgling engine.

"Hop to!" Alex shoved the door open and grabbing Edeen about the waist, Roque tossed her inside, following suit and Alex stomped the pedal to the floorboard. The truck heaved ahead, leaving Geschopf screeching out commands.

The back window exploded. A bullet whipped through Edeen's hair, breaking a hole in the front windscreen.

"Down!" Roque pulled Edeen to the side though there wasn't much room to maneuver.

Edeen's eyes were huge. Alex pulled the truck onto the main roadway through the village.

"Gun." Roque shouted, and Alex leaned forward over the large steering wheel, exposing the Enfield at the back of his waistband.

Roque grabbed it.

Angled it out the back.

Clouds of kicked-up dirt rolled behind them. No way

would he fire while still in the village proper.

A roar whined behind them. Out of the dust cloud emerged a Rolls Royce convertible a few meters from their tailpipe, and gaining.

Another bullet shrieked, plowing into the dashboard.

"Stoppen Sie feuern!"

"Faster," Roque shouted.

Alex's gaze snapped to his, annoyance flashing, then back to the road. The old lorry labored on, coughing and sputtering. They rolled onto the main roadway out of the village.

Edeen clutched the dashboard, knuckles white. "What manner of cart is this!"

"Lorry!" Roque and Alex growled out in unison. They were hit from behind. The truck groaned, front wheels lifting, then crashing back onto the road in a lurch.

Alex jerked the wheel, careening them to the right.

The Rolls followed, engine revving and plowed into them. They flew forward and back, bouncing against each other in the tight cab. A bullet hit the dashboard a centimeter from Edeen's fist and Roque growled.

Enough was enough.

Snarling, he jerked open the door and pivoted out, leaping into the truck bed and onto the front of the Rolls Royce. The driver, another *krampus*, shrieked, jerking the wheel. A shot went wild as they swerved off the roadway. Geschopf ripped the gun from the soldier.

"Don't shoot him!"

Roque tore the driver from the seat, throwing him out. The convertible bounced over him. Geschopf grabbed the wheel and Roque flew onto the seats after the second soldier in the back with a rifle.

"Roque, stop this," Geschopf shouted. "It's time for you to come home!" Geschopf got the car back onto the road.

Roque's head snapped up in disbelief. The soldier landed a kick to his chest that pushed. Roque into the gears stick. The Rolls lurched forward, gears squealing.

They hit . . . something, and the car tilted, rising up on one side, tires spinning in the air. Cursing, Geschopf tried to right it, but the Rolls Royce was already swerving too hard, dipping to its side.

Roque ducked down in the seats, rolling, tumbling through the air, pitching to a bone-jarring stop on the vehicle's side. The engine screeched, smoking, tires spinning.

Roque fell out to the ground, jarring every bone in his body. The soldier lay half beneath the crumbled side of the car, blood running from his lips, no heartbeat.

Pushing up to his knees, Roque shook his head to clear it.

And was grabbed from behind, hauled off his feet and spun to the gleaming red scales of a demi-dragon. Partially transformed, Geschopf survived the crash by transforming and leaping out of the rolling vehicle. Red scales rippled as Geschopf frowned, large snout cracking as Wulf reshaped back into a man. "Why do you run from me?" His dragon voice rasped, guttural and ancient, the purr of prehistoric magic beyond time.

Tires screeched on gravel.

Roque grabbed Geschopf's wrists, fighting to twist, pushing down the gut-wrenching fear. His legs floundered off the ground. He was a little boy again, caught up in Wulf's grip, torn away from all he knew and vulnerable.

Geschopf leaned in close. "We weren't finished, you and I. We will never be finished."

"Put him down," Edeen called out, and a terror more strong than what he'd ever felt as a child raged through Roque. Terror for Edeen. He didn't want Geschopf to so much as look upon her.

Both Roque and Geschopf swiveled sideways to see her. Wulf's slitted pupils expanded, taking her in.

Edeen stood just past the open door of the lorry yards away, Alex still at the wheel. She stood rigid, unafraid beneath the stare of one of the most truly heinous creatures upon the earth, pointing a German luger straight at them.

Geschopf smiled, revealing daggered teeth behind scaly lips. "Ah, the little empath. Come here, child."

"I told ye to put him down." She didn't bat an eye, though Roque felt the rapid frightened pace of her pulse.

Geschopf tsked as though she were a child. "First rule you'll learn: I'm in charge. Tell me what to do again and I'll break his—"

A shot barked out. Edeen stumbled back from the recoil. Geschopf gasped and stared at his shoulder, at the blossoming flow of violet blood.

The bullet.

The bullet engineered especially for Roque.

Especially for dragons.

Taking advantage of Geschopf's shock, Roque kicked out, getting out of the dragon's hold. He punched him in the gut, bending the powerful *Schwarze Klaue* over.

"Go, go!" Roque ran, grabbing Edeen by the arm and pulling her away, practically throwing her back into the truck as Alex stomped the accelerator.

As the lorry rattled down the roadway, Geschopf shouted, holding his shoulder and running after them until they climbed a hill, gaining speed when they came down the other side.

"Any idea where we're headed?"

"Away from here," Alex ground out. "Far as I can tell, we're on the arterial roadway to Dunoon."

Perfect. From Dunoon, they could catch a ferry across the Firth of Clyde and get to the Royal Naval shipyards at Greenock. No German, especially Geschopf would dare set foot in Greenock.

Chapter Nine

Edeen stared at the monstrosity of a ship. 'Twas all so strange, this century. And wondrous. Mechanisms. Engines. Mankind had created a magic of their own, powered by harnessing steam and minerals and fossils taken from the earth.

"What is it?"

After ditching the lorry in the city, this Dunoon, she and Roque waited in the shadow of a *factory* near the wharf while Alex went to secure passage across the Firth.

"Paddle steamer. The only one left for civilians that hasn't been conscripted by the Royal Navy." Roque took her hand and heat instantly flared between their palms. "Are you all right? None of this has been easy for you."

Edeen stared at the strange vessel, at the large wheel on her side and the tall smoke stacks. A longing for home, her time, her brothers and clan, crested over her. She needed to find a sorcerer to open a rift and send her home.

"I've managed it." Alex strode up the wharf. "I've booked three passages leaving within the hour. Captain doesn't usually ferry this late in the day, but he's agreed for us. We'll be in Greenock in just a few hours' time."

"Well done, Alex," Roque grinned.

Alex cocked his head. "I'll have you know being with the Ministry of Defense has its privileges. Well, come on then. Best get you both tucked away out of sight."

The paddle steamer was even more wondrous on board. A long flat-bottomed hull, it supported two levels of deckhouses with the captain's wheelhouse on top. Alex had shut Edeen and Roque in one and then had run off, saying something about food in passing.

He returned just before the paddle steamer shoved off with bags of food and odd assortments of clothing. Edeen stared through the window as large lumbering trolls lifted the gang-plank. She shook her head at the strange sight. Trolls, ghouls, creatures who thrived in their dark tunnels and caves, walked about the world openly.

She sat on the bed with Roque and Alex and devoured what the men called meat pies and tatties. Cramming the food in their mouths, none of them cared that the meat smeared their faces. 'Twas the most splendid meal Edeen had ever partaken of.

They were all so famished, no one spoke. Afterwards, Roque handed her a bundle of clothing and hustled her into a small attached type of garderobe with a large mirror.

At least she knew what to do with the bowl and pitcher of water, though she could not say the same about certain pieces of the clothing Roque had given her. Some of them resembled weapons more than something designed for a woman. Then again, being accustomed to

84

carrying a slim dirk in her belt, the women of this century must have need of their hidden weaponry as well, they were at war after all, though she could not fathom how to use it.

She sponged the dirt and sweat off herself, never so happy to get out of her ruined chemise, and set about figuring out the clothing.

Lifting the stretchy white piece up, 'twas obvious the cups were meant for her breasts, but she couldn't decide what the little round toggles hanging from some sort of rock sling had to do with smallclothes.

Puzzled, she tested the band, fascinated as it snapped back.

Getting into the top piece was simple enough. She tackled the short breeches-like small clothes next, sucking in a breath as she wiggled into them. Sweet peace, the cloth was constricting. 'Twas surely meant for torture.

The white blouse came next and Edeen marveled at the small clever fastening toggles that looked like small pearls, but felt entirely different. She shimmied into the short tight version of a gown, liking the less cumbersome freedom of movement her exposed legs gave her. She turned her attention next to the nearly sheer hose. How the flimsy material was to keep her legs warm she couldn't fathom, nor how to hold them up. There weren't any cross ties in the things Roque had given her.

Bleeding hell, they were too sheer to be of any use

anyway. She left the stockings on the counter beside the water bowl and pushed the door open, peering into the room. She suddenly felt self-conscious. What if she didn't measure up to the women of Roque's time? The thought startled her.

Why should she bloody well care? She was going back to her own time, but . . . Roque lounged on the bed, long legs crossed at the ankles, the empty wrappings of their hasty meal around him. His head craned up as though he felt her presence—he most likely did—and everything inside Edeen quieted.

A powerful yearning washed over her heart.

He sat up, looking her over and Edeen felt self-conscious again. She stepped into the room. If anything, Roque's smile deepened and Edeen melted. His gaze tracked over her form and down to her bare legs. Her heart sank. Mayhap she had made a blunder by not putting on the long stockings.

Coming off the bed, he came to her and took her hand. Heat instantly sparked between them.

"You're beautiful."

Edeen's cheeks burned at the compliment. She had many would-be suitors exclaim the same thing before her brothers harried them away, yet no such endearment pierced her soul in quite the same manner.

Her heart pounded. Her skin felt flush.

"Where's Alex?"

"Went to see about a radio."

"Ray-dee-oh," she repeated the strange new word and Roque smiled, guiding her to sit on the only chair in the small deckhouse.

"Allow me."

He picked up a brush from a side table and walked around behind her. Long fingers worked through the tangles in her hair. Edeen could barely breathe. Heat washed across her skin.

"Roque?" She swallowed, afraid to ask. Afraid to learn the answer.

"Mmmm?"

The hair brush pulled through her hair. Edeen's pulse picked up.

"What's become of my brothers?"

The brush stilled. A terrible throbbing started behind her throat and eyes. "I know 'tis something horrible." Her voice caught. "Ye and Alex are keen to not speak of it."

She felt Roque sigh. Putting the brush aside, he came around the chair to kneel in front of her, dark head down.

Gods, nay. What had happened to her brothers?

Roque took her hands. Hers were so cold, his felt scorching.

"Sweetheart." He lifted those dark fathomless eyes to hers. "We don't know much. The histories are quiet on what exactly befell the last four guardians of Clan Limont. But I will tell you what I do know."

Last four guardians. Edeen nodded, her throat too raw to speak.

Roque's fingers curled around hers. "The sibling guardians battled a witch upon a hill." Roque's head canted to the side, eyes narrowed. "Do you remember?"

Vividly. For her it had happened a mere day ago, not seven hundred years in the past. She nodded.

"Something happened between you and the witch. You were caught within a deep slumber that even a sorcerer as powerful as Toren Limont could not awaken you from."

The witch Aldreth had unleashed her powers upon Toren. She was going to kill him. Full of fear and anger, Edeen ran at her, thinking that if only she could touch the witch with her empathic gift, she could throw Aldreth back into her memories, throw her off the attack. Aldreth was hurting Toren when he was already so battered and weak, she had to do something. But it had all gone horribly wrong.

The witch's magic had attacked Edeen's essence, a darkness latching onto her gift, then . . . nothing.

Until she awoke to Roque hovering over her and a scorching ache in her neck.

"The sorcerer tried everything he knew. He searched for years for a way to awaken you." Roque told her.

Edeen startled. "Years? So Toren survived the witch? They defeated Aldreth."

Roque frowned at her. "Luv, you know they're all long gone."

"In this time." She rose, moving around him. "I intend to go back."

Roque stood, placing his fists at his waist. "How?"

"Find a sorcerer, convince him to open a time rift . . . " Her words tapered off at the sadness that crossed Roque's features.

"Edeen, there are no more sorcerers."

Terror sank like teeth into her throat. "But . . ."

Roque came to her, took her hand and spoke gently. "I'm so sorry. When your clan passed into the Shadowrood, they took the Fae's magic with them. Your brother Toren was the last of the sorcerers."

"But there's magic here. I've seen it. The ghouls and trolls. And you . . ."

Roque nodded. "Your brothers didn't defeat the witch."

Edeen shifted back, but Roque's grasp kept her in place. "The witch took Shaw and with him a new magic, dark magic, filled the void the Fae's magic left. Dark magic overcame the world. Have you not seen it here?"

"Shaw? But he took our people into the Shadowrood."

Roque shook his head. "Shaw came to the hill. The witch captured him, turned him, and dark magic consumed the world."

This time, Edeen did pull away and he let her go.

"Nay. Shaw would never give in."

Sorrow filled Roque's eyes. "He may have been forced, or gone insane through torture. We don't know. But he did give in. Darkness overcame. Ghouls. Trolls. Gremlins. Wizards." His arms spread wide. "Vampires...every evil magical creature once relegated to shadows roams the earth freely."

"This Hitler? He too is of dark magic?"

A faint smile touched Roque's mouth. "It turns out humankind is capable of creating a far worse monster than vampires or ghouls."

Edeen covered her mouth. Tremors rolled through her.

Roque took a step toward her. "I am so sorry. I would do whatever I could if there was a way to get you home. I promise you I would."

A low roaring pressed against her temples. Her vision went cloudy. Shaw turned, he turned, destroying his soul. Dark magic overcame the world, and Toren and Charity? Oh gods, Col . . . Edeen swayed.

She was suddenly lifted into strong arms. A steady heart beat next to her ear. Lips kissed her forehead and Roque whispered, "Shh, shhh, luv. You're all right."

But she wasn't. She was lost and alone, her family gone. Tears blurred her vision. "I cannot get home. I . . ." She hiccupped. "I cannot help my brothers."

She curled her fist in Roque's shirt. "Roque. What

happened to them? Ye must tell me. What of Charity?"

"Shh, you've learned enough for now."

"I'm not a child. Tell me."

His sigh rumbled through his chest. He sat on the bed, keeping her in his lap. His hand smoothed down her hair.

"Toren used the last of his strength to preserve you within the smugglers cave. It was a powerful spell." He shook his head, his chin rubbing across the top of her head. "After that we don't know. We know the healer was with him and they simply disappeared off the pages of history."

Edeen sniffled. "He did not attempt to save Shaw?"

"It was too late. Shaw too powerful . . ."

"And Col?"

Roque stiffened. Heat shot off his skin. Edeen snapped her head up to face him. "Col?"

Roque's eyes shimmered. She glimpsed a grief of his own in them, exposed and unbearably defenseless. "Nothing more was mentioned of him after the battle on Crunfathy Hill. We assume the witch killed him."

Everything stopped.

Col, her youngest brother, light of their family, gone?

A low keen escaped her throat. *Col, Col.* Low tremors hissed beneath her skin. Roque folded her within his strength, a warm hand cupping the back of her head. She turned her face into his chest and sobbed.

Everything they'd set out to stop, had happened anyway. . . . And Col was dead.

Gods, they were all dead, rotted to dust long ago while she slept.

Tears burned her eyes, choked her throat, dampened Roque's shirt. He crooned soft assurances she couldn't make out above her own pain-filled gasping.

She was lost. She was lost. She was lost.

But not alone.

She didn't feel alone in Roque's arms.

Seeking, she was not sure what, she pressed closer to him, listened to the strong certain beat of his heart, felt the heat of him shimmer off his skin. Her palm flattened above his heart—

Images poured into her essence, potent emotions full of young bravado, and fear.

A young boy with a dark fringe of bangs obscuring his eyes screamed, dropping beside a pale broken woman.

"You killed her!"

Lunging up, he flew at a man, fists pounding into his chest. "You killed her you killed her." Fire erupted, engulfing both man and boy, though neither burned, their skin unmarred beneath licking flames.

The man slapped out and the child fell to the ground beside the dead woman. The fire from the boy jumped to the woman. She exploded in flames, catching on fire quickly as though she were made of dry kindling. Vampire.

The boy screamed, trying to pat out the flames consuming the dead woman. His young gaze snapped up, hazy behind tears, and Edeen recognized Geschopf.

"She would never have given you up." Geschopf picked up the wailing boy, hauling him over his shoulder and walked away as the beautiful child stretched out his arms. "Mama, Mama."

The vision wrenched away, though Edeen reached for it, clawed to get it back, to have control over her gift once more.

"Edeen!"

Roque held her by the arms and gave her a little shake. "Edeen!"

She nodded, pulling in an unstable breath.

"What was that?"

She winced, hand going to her head.

"Your abilities?"

She nodded.

"They're coming back?"

"I'm not sure. I had no control of it." She looked into his face, glimpsing the young boy in him.

"What did you see?" His voice was uncertain.

"You. As a child. Geschopf took you from your mother."

The air filled with charged energy. The giant paddle wheel churned outside their deckhouse.

Roque's stared hard and then his features softened

and he smoothed a lock of hair off her cheek. "I'm glad for you. Glad you have your gift back."

"Though it makes me more of a threat to your people."

"Or an aide. With or without your gifts, Edeen, Hitler won't get near you."

Chapter Ten

Roque held Edeen close while the last of the tremors rolled through her. She had seen a piece of his past, a part he kept buried and separate. Although Alex knew some of what happened to him as a child, Roque wouldn't share details. He knew It had been in his official dossier and as his military handler, Alex would have seen it.

Yet Edeen's gift had flown straight to the worse moment of his life and somehow that had felt right as though she were the only person in this messed-up existence he *could* share it with.

Frowning, he tried to collect his feelings. She felt right in his arms. She was right. She had nestled her way under his skin and gods help him, he wanted to keep her there.

He held her while her pulse slowed, drifting into the soft cadence of sleep and then he laid her gently on the bed, smiling when she murmured and turned over on her side.

Closing his eyes, he allowed himself to fall into the soft rasp of her even breathing, the soft hum of blood drifting through her veins. She was lovely. When she'd stepped from the washroom, barefoot and tousled-hair, he could barely breathe. He wanted her so badly it was a physical ache. *Treasure*.

Beneath them, the hull pushed through the water, another type of pulse, steady and as old as the earth that had seen battles and wars, yet still remained.

Where the hell was Alex?

It didn't take this long to radio in to Greenock.

Instantly alert, Roque cracked the door open and the salty air ruffled his hair. They were close to the shipyards. He could make out dark outlines of boats and buildings against the darkening sky, quiet and surreal, all lights extinguished for the evening's blackout.

The scent of troll grew heavier as he made his way up to the wheelhouse. Nasty smelly beasts, their scent covered everything and was almost too much for his senses. He supposed he should be grateful since a troll's vision was keen enough to traverse the Firth after dark in a blackout. A human captain would never have risked crossing this late.

Roque stood outside the wheelhouse, listening for irregularities. The captain was inside; his five-chambered heart beating heavily, almost too loud for a vampire's sensitive hearing. Between the stink and the noise, a throbbing pressure was building behind Roque's eyes. The sooner they got to Greenock, the better. Two more trolls were near the bottom aft, most likely searching the waters for shoals. The heartbeats of the three trolls nearly overpowered all the other heartbeats, a few humans, a few non-humans.

Roque concentrated, searching for Alex's rhythm beneath the noise.

He found it, surprisingly faint, just inside the wheelhouse. Roque looked through the window, finding only the captain inside at the wheel, nothing out of the ordinary. Just the troll and Alex who he could not see. Something was off.

Quietly, he lifted the latch, ready to burst inside when a soft snick penetrated the quiet.

A tiny light fluttered in the breeze and went out.

Roque froze.

Slowly, he turned.

Geschopf came around the back of the wheelhouse and leaned against the railing, gloved hands cupped around his mouth to shield a cigarette from the wind.

Of course. A dragon's heart ran quieter, smaller, easy to hide beneath the clamor and stench of trolls. Geschopf had been on the paddle steamer all along.

"You should put that out." Roque's voice came out steadier than he'd thought. "Blackout and all."

Geschopf's lips turned down like a shrug. He took a long drag and then flicked the cigarette over the side into the water.

Roque watched it disappear, his heart racing with violence. Geschopf was so close, within reach. Edeen was just below, asleep and vulnerable in their deckhouse. And Alex . . . what had Geschopf done to Alex?

"I want you back, Roquemore."

Roque flinched, not expecting that. Acid rose, coating his tongue. His neck and wrists itched, phantom remainders of restraints.

"No." His tone scraped raw.

Geschopf tsked, the same way he had when Roque was a young man right before *die Schwarze Klaue* tested how many fingers he could break before Roque lost control of his fire. Small beads of perspiration dotted Roque's forehead.

"We were not finished, you and I." Geschopf's smile was patient.

Roque squared his shoulders. "We finished long ago. I escaped."

Geschopf took a pack of cigarettes from his front pocket and tapped it in his palm. "Did you?" The *Sturmhauptführer* smiled, seeing that Roque understood. "A field study, shall we say. To see what could be achieved without force or restraint."

A tremor rolled through him. He was going to be sick. The life he'd built so carefully on his own, the good he thought he'd achieved with his unique skills, that he'd so desperately tried to take the ugliness Geschopf had put him through and make something good out of it. All of that had been carefully studied by the monster before him.

Geschopf pulled out another cigarette. "I could have reeled you in at any time."

So why now? Why make his presence known now? Roque's mouth tightened, knowing the answer. Edeen. And he had led the Black Claw right to her. Roque took a step forward.

"I wouldn't." Geschopf placed the unlit cigarette between his lips. "You want to rip my throat out with your bare hands. Good. Keep that fire in your soul. Hatred feeds you strength."

Roque did hate him. Flame hissed across his skin, reflecting in Geschopf's dark eyes. Wulf swallowed, drunk on controlling Roque's abilities.

"Come." Geschopf reached across Roque to grasp the door latch. "We've much to discuss, and you, have choices to make." He pulled the door open and waited for Roque to enter.

Stiffly, Roque stepped into the wheelhouse. It felt like giving away a piece of his soul.

The troll glanced down at them. Alex was a mess just inside, huddled in the corner behind the door, face torn and bloodied.

"Alex!"

Roque went to his knees, but the troll captain quickly stepped between them.

Strong arms suddenly grabbed him from behind. Geschopf pulled him back against him, and nodded to the captain. "The Lieutenant's usefulness is ended. Get rid of him."

"No!" Roque reacted swiftly, jabbing a fist into Geschopf's throat and throwing himself at the troll's back, already blocking the door

Unbothered by Roque's strength, the behemoth hauled Alex out the door and pitched him over the rail. The splash was lost in the churning of the large wheel.

Roque shoved the troll and braced to jump.

Geschopf's voice rattled across the air. "Save the boy or save the girl."

It felt like a lightning bolt speared him to the spot, petrifying the moment. Roque's heart came to a stuttering stop.

He twisted back.

Geschopf was straightening, a hand at his neck, his voice rough. "Go on. Jump. I'll find you again. I'll always find you."

He couldn't leave Edeen to this monster.

Heartsick, Roque stared down into the cold churning water. Without a word, he went back into the wheelhouse, grabbed the supply kit off the wall, and found the flashlight. Clicking it on, he strode back outside, and jerked the life ring off the railing. He tied the flashlight to it all the while Geschopf watched with a bemused grin. Forever studying Roque, examining his every move and motivation with a scientist's eye. Roque embraced the fire boiling within him.

Geschopf could burn in hell.

Finished, Roque threw the life ring far out into the water, watching the flashlight dip and bob, a small beacon in a gulf of blackness.

He hoped Alex could see it, even knowing his friend was far behind them. He hoped Alex was still alive, still fighting, not crushed in the giant wheel or swept beneath the steamer's giant wake.

Geschopf chuckled behind his shoulder. "You still cling to hope . . . after all these years. At the forefront to aid your little allied friends. It is a weakness, you know. When you have the potential to seize so much power..." Geschopf sighed, truly disappointed.

"Let go of me," Edeen called from below.

Roque moved to go to her.

"Remain here, Roque. We wouldn't want the empath to come to harm."

"You need her," Roque snarled. "Hitler wants her."

"Her skills. A broken arm won't hinder that."

The dragon in Roque roared to the surface, protective. Possessive. Edeen was his. *Mate*, the dragon hissed.

The fact that he'd just claimed her didn't warrant reflection in his current state. His blood churned. Fire erupted along his arms.

"Good, Roquemore," Geschopf praised. "Unleash the rage."

Geschopf's men prodded Edeen up the steps and flames roared anew at the sight of her, rippling across Roque's shoulders, his chest. Discoloration from a slap marred her cheek. Barefoot, hair disheveled and loose, she glared at the men. He glared at the men. *Shite*, not men. Vampires. Geschopf had brought his vampires.

Ablaze, Roque rocked forward, intent on throwing the first vampire over the rail or simply set him to burn.

"*Brechen ihr Schlüsselbein.*" Geschopf called out. "Snap her collarbone."

Roque stopped, and immediately quenched his flames. What was left of his shirt burned around him.

"Your control has improved." Geschopf cocked his head and went into the wheelhouse, not bothering to make sure he was followed. He knew Roque had no choice.

Chapter Eleven

The vampire steered Edeen into the troll captain's little room. She immediately sought out Roque. He stood stiffly on the other side of the large wheel, hands clenched into fists by his sides. The soldiers, vampires, who had taken her from her room flanked her. One kept his hand curled around her upper arm, keeping her in place.

Roque's gaze traveled over her, no doubt looking for injuries. Scant little remained of his charred shirt. Scraps and threads he had not bothered to whisk off.

Geschopf moved in front of Roque and dipped his head graciously to her. "My Lady."

Edeen stayed still. This was the man, the monster, who had hurt Roque. Countless times.

"Her gift is gone," Roque said suddenly. "She's of no use to you."

Geschopf angled his head, studying her. "She better hope that's not true." Then more gently to Edeen. "Does he lie?"

Edeen looked from one man to the other, hoping to gauge from their expressions the right way to respond and found no aide there. With one touch she could ferret out and supply Geschopf with all the answers he wanted.

"Nay, he does not lie. When I awakened, my gift was gone, buried, but it is returned."

Geschopf's brow rose. "Completely?"

She did not know.

Her talents were hazy and fragmented. Random thoughts and memories she was unable to guide. Her gift was there, but she did not have the control over it she once commanded. "Yes."

Roque did not move a muscle.

Something within Geschopf's dark eyes glinted. "Show me. Place your hands on young Roquemore here and tell me what you see."

"How do you suppose I know my gifts are back?" She snapped. She had feared Aldreth, was enraged by what the witch had put her brother through, but this man... Aldreth craved power. He drank torture and pain like wine. She wrenched her arm out of the vampire's grasp and took a step to the center of the small window-filled room. "I've already touched Roque. I know enough."

"Then tell me." Geschopf took a step toward her, a towering, solid presence. Behind him, Roque shifted, balancing his weight forward. A stance so like Shaw's it hurt.

Geschopf's hot breath washed over her. "Tell me Roque's secrets."

Edeen stilled the urge to cringe back. She met

Geschopf's gaze flatly. "You do not need me to reveal what you already know. He hates you. He'll kill you if he can."

Amusement played over the Black Claw's lips. "It does not take an empath to see that."

"You murdered his mother." Edeen lifted her chin. "Stole him, tortured him for years."

Geschopf nodded. "To make him stronger. To take him to the excesses of his abilities." He lifted a strand of Edeen's hair. It took everything within her to remain still. "I can teach you to strengthen your gift."

Edeen swallowed. Dear gods, he truly believed he had helped Roque.

She tugged her head away and her hair sifted through his gloves like water. "Ye would put me under yer lash? Bind me to yer rack? To enhance my abilities?"

Roque's jaw clenched.

Geschopf's mouth twisted in a wry smile. "Pain is a powerful conductor."

"I think not." She folded her arms. "I do not wish to endure yer teaching methods."

Geschopf laughed at that, clearly enjoying their exchange. "Most people do not." He leaned closer, his voice low. "Most people do not have buried talents that only pain may reveal."

Heart pounding, Edeen stepped away to get out from under his direct stare. She went over to the counter, housing the wheel and several other strange objects. "I have another proposal."

A dark brow lifted, smoothing lines from Geschopf's cheek. "Go on." His tone was coddling, spoken to someone who had no choice in the matter.

Edeen took in a breath. "I will go with you willingly. I will do whatever this Hitler needs of me."

Geschopf's gaze narrowed. She had surprised him. "No moral issues? Roquemore has not fed you his propaganda?"

Edeen shook her head. "This is not my war. I am adrift in this world, alone. My family gone. Why would I not help those who have the means to keep me safe, who can provide for me?"

Geschopf inclined his head. "I see your point. You're more intelligent than I could have hoped." A feral glimmer sparked his eyes, prepared to test her further. "What of Roquemore? You know we have history. Are you willing to let me resume his *training* and still honor our deal?"

"Honestly, I would rather you not, but do I really have a choice in the matter?"

He chuckled.

She dug in to her resolve. "What do I have to do with him?" She didn't bat an eye. Couldn't. "Do what ye must as long as I survive intact." It physically hurt to say it. Nausea filled her belly.

Geschopf's jagged smile widened. He turned to

Roque to study his reaction.

Roque gave nothing away, his body stiff, but whether over the promise of more torture or Edeen's betrayal wasn't clear.

Geschopf turned back, extending his forearm. "Madam, we have a deal."

Without hesitation, Edeen took his hand and slapped her other pam to his chest, unleashing her pent-up essence. It flowed into him like an arrow.

Geschopf screamed. His arms locked up tight. Edeen drove her essence into his heart, an ugly shriveled black thing.

At the edge of her awareness she sensed Roque fly past her, heard grunts before that all dissolved away and she was with Geschopf, reliving moments, the world on fire, and she screamed.

Chapter Twelve

Experiences flooded Edeen, charged with fear turned to hatred that spun on the pinnacle of madness. Geschopf's life was horror, terrifying and harsh, his own father mad, driven by power, heaping abuse upon abuse upon Wulf until Geschopf plunged his claw through his father's throat and became the new Black Claw, far more creative and lethal. Geschopf broke and remade a parade of magical wielders. They flashed before Edeen in a mockery of life. Torn flesh, flayed muscles, broken, beaten, terrorized beneath her hands—Geschopf's hands—enhanced, empowered, better, stronger, more capable. Pride washed through her. So proud, she, *no he*, was so proud of what he had made of them.

Edeen wanted to vomit. She tried to flee, escape the trap of his madness. She didn't want any part of this. Oh gods, Roque's innocent young face flashed before her. Year's worth of torment as the young man grew to adulthood under Wulf's tutelage. Her essence wept, struggled to get free. What Geschopf had done to him, harder and so much worse than the others, his special pet project, his beautiful beautiful powerful boy.

Beloved and despised by Wulf.

Dragons awake from their millennial slumber to walk the earth in the skin of a man for decades, spilling seed, before returning to the bowels of earth to slumber for a thousand years more. Some offspring between dragon and human retain their draconic abilities, as did Geschopf from his dragon grandsire, where his own hated father did not.

Yet the direct offspring between dragon and vampire...envy and pride for Roque coursed through Geschopf's emotions as intertwined as strands of hemp. He loved him like his own and hated him for it, a sick twisted fervor of a disturbed mind.

The truth lifted right from Geschopf's innermost emotions. Roquemore was dragon spawned. Joining of vampire and dragon. The only one of his kind in existence.

If she, nay, Geschopf, if Geschopf could force Roque to transform, as a dragon Roque would lose all human compassion, regress to his animalistic cravings, as Wulf had, she realized. Geschopf needed Roque to become the dragon in order to master him fully. Her stomach roiled.

There was a rough grating sound and the images swirled. Experiences came at her faster, ripping through her soul, ripping her apart.

A new leader arose, blood and death fluttering behind his heels. A reign of terror, of unimaginable cruelty. His own people rounded up, murdered, experimented upon.

Heaps of decimated, ruined bodies trailed his essence like mounds of blood. Darkness and hatred covered the continent beneath hatred's shroud.

Geschopf admired him, this mad *dictator* who dared conceive of a race as strong and pure as what the Black Claw himself envisioned.

Edeen screamed to get free of the nightmare. The darkness of Geschopf's spirit held her essence, burrowing like a taproot into her gut.

Sick, sick, she was going to be sick, whirling, she fled through Geschopf's emotions, finding death and horror at every turn. There was no place to go, nothing but blood, blood, blood.

Abruptly she was jerked away, coming back to her body in a painful thrust.

Geschopf writhed on the floor, shrieking, gloves tearing at his scalp as she was pulled backwards away from him. She was being carried, a strong arm pressed across her stomach, hurting, making the need to spew even greater.

They went out the door, past blood-coated vampires sprawled on the floor. One of their heads was missing, torn off.

She wondered where the captain was. He should be steering the boat, shouldn't he?

Hysteric laughter bubbled in her throat. She was set on her feet. Roque's face swam into view, his mouth working, though whatever he was saying came out echoey.

. . . off this boat . . . Geschopf won't . . . down long . . .

He took her roughly by the shoulders. "Edeen!"

There was shouting, the slapping of boots on metal steps. Edeen blinked up at Roque, trying to make sense of it and felt like weeping. *Oh Roque, what he did to you*.

Shouts, grating noises. Roque's face swung away. "Bleeding hell. There's too many—"

Edeen felt herself lifted and then they were flying through the dark sky until the cold, cold ocean reached up and swallowed them whole.

Chapter Thirteen

"Edeen, come on. Are you with me, luv?" He pulled her through the water, moving away from the slushing paddle steamer. He didn't know what had happened between them when Edeen grabbed ahold of Geschopf's chest. They'd both frozen, caught in some sort of spell it seemed, and it had scared the shite out of him. He'd reacted swiftly, taking out the two vampires and snatched Edeen away.

And he would wager Geschopf wouldn't be down long, but searching the water for them even now.

Roque could get them to shore. He had enough stamina and endurance for the both of them, but something was wrong with Edeen. "Come on, Treasure. Show me that you're still with me." He treaded water for her. "Edeen?"

A wave swept over them.

Edeen's eyes jerked open, tracked around the water for a bit, until finally focusing.

"Oh, Roque." It was the most heart-wrenching wonderful sound he'd ever heard. His blood roared to life again.

"Geschopf . . ." Her chin trembled and there was

heartbreak in her eyes. "He's done the most horrible things." Her voice cracked. "To you. To so many others. And, and, this Hitler—" She broke on a sob as a wave dashed over their heads.

He pulled her in closer. "I know, I know."

"Ye do not know. None of ye know what he's done to his own people. 'Tis horrible. I hate this world. I hate it. 'Tis dark and ugly. Mortals have become monsters. I want to go home."

"I know, I know. It's going to be okay. You're going to be all right."

Her sobbing slowed and she finally nodded. Pride filled his chest. Gods, he loved her.

Roque?" her voice was quiet. Water splashed over them, lifting them in their roll. "I did not mean any of those things I said to him."

He smiled, though they were so close together she couldn't see it. "I never considered that you did." He kissed her forehead, found her skin to be cold. She was freezing, the sea water stealing her strength. "You were very cunning and brave."

He drew from the fire in his core, letting it flow through his skin, pulling her close so his warmth would revive her.

Edeen pressed her head more heavily into the crook of his neck. "I would never make a deal with Geschopf."

Roque's heart dropped like a stone. He pulled back to look at her. "Yes, you will. If something happens to me, if

113

we're separated, anything at all, Edeen, you make that deal. You do whatever you have to do to stay alive. Promise me that."

Her eyes were huge, shining in the moonlight. "Nay, Roque. I cannot—"

"You can. You stay alive. You survive. And I will come for you. But you stay alive."

They stared at each other. Small waves lifted and dropped them. His heat reviving her, lips trembling, she nodded.

"Just do not make it come to that." She rested her head back onto his shoulder. Her breath was cold on his wet neck.

"With all that I'm capable of," he quietly vowed and felt her stiffen.

"Gods, nay. Alex, we left Alex."

He'd do anything not to tell her, but she was a woman who didn't take to being placated. "Geschopf had him tossed overboard." He left out that the lad had been badly beaten first. "He's strong and capable. Keep faith for him."

Edeen nodded against him. Whether she believed him or not remained unspoken.

"We need to make the shore." He pulled her around to his back, arranging her arms around his shoulders. "I need you to hang on."

"I can swim."

"I know, but it will be much faster this way. Trust me."

"I do," she said quietly and nothing in his existence had ever meant as much.

He squeezed her hands, ready to begin his swim, when he heard it.

The heavy halting drone of bombers. His gaze wrenched up to the dark sky, the booming roar of engines close overhead. At least fifty bombers passing over them, using the bright moonlight as a guide.

Mother of God, Roque's heart lodged in his throat.

German aircraft. The *Luftwaffe* headed directly toward Greenock. Toward the shipyards.

The sleeping inhabitants had no warning.

Sound the sirens, he willed the watchman, or anyone, to see what came for them.

"What are those?" Edeen whispered.

Roque's tone came out strangled, barely croaking out one word, "Death."

The first glow of red hit Greenock like a flash of sunset, casting buildings and spired churches into dark shadowed reliefs.

Bombs whistled down from the planes, exploding, flowering in blazes of horrible light.

Shrill notes of the sirens went off, carrying over the water. Searchlights swept the sky and from across the river Clyde the ba-boom of anti-aircraft rumbled.

All Roque could do was swim. Swim with everything he had to Greenock.

Chapter Fourteen

She was numb. The water had grown cold again and she felt like a bag of unfeeling flesh pressed against Roque's back, though she didn't tell him.

He'd been swimming for hours, yet even his astonishing endurance must have limits and Edeen wouldn't take from his reserves because she was cold. She adjusted her grip around his shoulders, flexing her water-logged wrinkled fingers.

The sky was lightening into the gray of pre-dawn. She could make out the ships and buildings that lined the approaching shore and several pointed spires that in her time signified a keep's tower, possibly a church. She wondered if they still meant the same.

She recognized the long sandbar that marked the tail of an estuary that poured into the Firth, having visited the small fishing village that once occupied this shoreline a fortnight ago. Centuries ago, she corrected herself, her heart as frozen as her body. It was so quiet and still as though the events of the night were only a horrible dream. Flying beasts dropping fire and destruction from the sky.

Like dragons, ancient serpents, the true sleepers through time.

Edeen felt the muscles of Roque's back move beneath her cheek, a true dragon.

She squinted, her eyes sore and gritty from the sea, toward everything that had changed. There was too much loss. Too much to mourn. Her heart was heavy as though it too had soaked up too much water and was pulling her down to the depths of the ocean.

"Edeen?" Roque's hand came back around and tapped her hip. "Are you with me, lass?"

"Aye," she answered dutifully.

He jostled her thigh. "Stay awake, Treasure. We're almost ashore."

"Not a treasure. Nummm." Her eyes hurt, so she let them slide closed.

"None of that, sweetheart. I can feel you not trying."

"Bloody vampire," she used his favorite oath. His bloody rotting senses would pick out the slackened beating of her pulse.

A chuckle filled his tone. "That's my girl."

Except she wasn't. She did not have anyone she belonged to. She had not lied to Geschopf about there being no one left in the world that belonged to her either.

And this world was horrible and frightening, where machines filled the sky and rained fire upon slumbering innocents. Even Aldreth had not wielded a power so terrible.

The air around her warmed and she realized she was

no longer floating lifelessly in the sea bay, but carried in Roque's arms.

His legs splashed through water as he carried her to shore, the fire of his body warming hers.

"I am well." She pushed to be let down, but her arm had little strength left. She would not take more from Roque. He was exhausted.

He would not let her down, but stared off to his left. "Huh. The shipyards took little damage."

The same could not be said for the rest of what she could make out in the low light of Greenock.

"Stay right there," a young voice called out. "D-dinna move."

A young boy stood near a boulder, holding one of those long *guns* in shaking hands. He was caked in dirt, light hair mussed, his cheek splattered with blood. "Are ye a downed pilot, then?"

"Son," Roque spoke very calmly and set Edeen onto her feet, stepping out around her, which she did not mind as it was unlikely the child's weapon carried Geschopf's dragon-killing *bullets*. Her legs felt wobbly, but she remained upright.

Roque held his palms out, placating, though with his speed, he could just as easily disarm the lad. "If I were a pilot, I'd be in uniform. Nor would I have a woman with me."

The boy's face crumbled. His shoulders sagged.

"There's no bullets anyway." He rubbed his wet nose across his dirty sleeve. "Can you . . . can you . . . I need help. The house, our house, it fell on us. My sister . . ." he wailed.

Edeen and Roque looked at each other, then back to the boy. Roque nodded. "Show us where."

They hurried through the dark streets. Entire lines of houses, or possibly a long keep were damaged. Walls shattered, the masonry collapsed into rooms. Farther away, a spire tower was on fire. They passed a woman in her nightclothes, shouting for her husband to get up. He lay at her feet, his neck at an impossible angle, eyes open to the smoke-choked sky.

Looking away, Edeen hurried after Roque and the boy, watching her footing through the debris and broken glass as she had no shoes.

Roque strode ahead, shoulders thrown forward in grim determination.

They came to another row of houses, half-fallen in. The glass from all the windows had scattered and stuck into walls and furniture.

The boy started climbing beneath a titled piece of wall, but Roque pulled him back. "Whoa, whoa, little man."

"But she's in there somewhere. We were sleeping." Tears streaked through the dirty blood on his cheeks. "I have to find her."

"And we will." Roque got on a knee to get face-to-face

with the boy. "The more people go in there, the more chance of things falling on her. I know right where she is. I can feel her." Roque smiled, purposely revealing the long pointed tips of two of his teeth.

The child's head canted, his brows pushing together. "You're a . . . a vampire?"

Roque nodded.

"Not supposed to talk to them." The boy frowned. "You can hear her heart beating? So she's alive?"

"She's alive," Roque assured. "And I can get her."

Thank you, mister. Thank you." His chin quivered and he swayed like the relief took away the last reserve he'd been clinging to.

Roque caught him by the arms. "What's your sister's name?"

"Margaret."

"All right. Stay here and I'll get her." With that, Roque ducked through the broken wall.

Edeen came to the boy, resting her arm across his bony shoulders. He surprised her by leaning in close as they listened to rubble scraping and being thrown aside, craning their necks at every glimpse of movement inside.

"What's your name?" Edeen asked quietly.

The boy sniffled. "Thomas."

"Thomas, where's yer parents?"

"My dad mans the radar aerial at the gun site across the river. "My mam . . ." His eyes got a hollow look to them.

120

"Her room was over there." He pointed to a sunken pile of rubble. "It's gone."

Edeen squeezed his shaking shoulder.

Black fabric covered the windows of a house across the street, which had taken no damage at all.

"Edeen," Roque called out. "I need your help."

"Stay here," she told Thomas. "If anyone comes by, ask them for help." Without question, she crawled into what looked like the aftermath of a hurricane.

Large pieces of wall and roof had collapsed inward. Pieces of glass were embedded in everything. Roque had made good progress in clearing most of the debris from around a young woman, though a large slab slanted across her legs while smaller chunks were sliding in around her.

Roque had his back against what looked like a large boulder, but must be a piece of wall or ceiling, his legs braced, features pinched with effort. Edeen followed the boulder's intended path and swallowed. He was the only thing keeping it from crushing the girl.

"I shifted the wrong piece, and . . ." he gave a slight shrug.

No need for further explanation. Edeen hiked the tight wet skirt up to climb carefully over slabs and broken furniture to get to the young woman. She was awake, her eyes overly bright and glassy in the dirt-caked face.

Edeen smiled for her. "Margaret, don't worry. We'll

have ye free in a moment." She started scooping chunks of wall and fist-sized rocks away.

"But that stone will cr-crush . . ."

"Nay, Margaret. Not while he holds it. Roque will not let harm come to ye. He promised yer brother."

"Thomas? He's okay?"

"He's fine. Worried for you so ye must be brave."

Margaret nodded and Edeen pulled more dirt and stones away, freeing the lass's upper body. The girl's arm moved, a good token, though the other one remained still and lifeless.

"What of my mam?"

Edeen stilled, but recovered her composure, testing a piece of splintered wood to see if it would make anything fall before removing it. "I do not know."

Tears slid down Margaret's face and into her hair, leaving streaks along her dirty face.

Edeen stopped digging to take her hand. "Are ye in pain?" Of course she was. She glanced back at Roque still pressed against the boulder. His limbs shook. Sweat ran along his hairline. He'd already been exhausted. It seemed hopeless, yet looking at Roque, at the force of his spirit, she knew they could do this.

Giving up on Margaret was not a consideration.

"My legs hurt. Really awful."

Edeen rubbed her wrist, feeling helpless and overwhelmed. She did not have the strength to lift the slab off of Margaret and trying to dig beneath made it sink and shift. "That's well, Margaret. Pain is sometimes good to let ye know everything still works. 'Tis what my brothers say."

"You have brothers?"

"Aye. Three and not a pound of sense between them." A swift ache flooded her chest. She wished they were here. Together her brothers would lift the debris and save the lass. Then Charity would heal her. Unshed tears blurred Edeen's vision.

Margaret's fingers curled around hers. "I'm going to die, aren't I?"

"Nay, Margaret, I will not let ye."

The lass smiled at that and nodded.

"Edeen," Roque's voice strained with effort.

She looked up and found several men crawling beneath the partially fallen wall.

Not men. Gremlins. She blinked, having never seen the thin creatures even in her own time. They wore black iron helmets with bands of gold that bent their pointed ears downward and she'd never been happier to see anyone in her life.

"Lad said you could use a hand in here."

Nodding like a drunkard, Edeen nearly sagged with relief.

The lead gremlin took his helmet off and placed it on Margaret's head. Though thin and fragile seeming, the gremlins were strong. In no time they had the boulder secured with rope and Margaret freed and her and her brother whisked away, hopefully to some kind of Healer Sorceress.

Outside the destroyed house, Edeen sank down on, she wasn't sure what it was, a broken chair? She was exhausted, her limbs shaky and weak.

Roque lowered beside her, and rested his head in his hands. She felt low tremors run through him.

The bowed legs of a gremlin stood before them. Roque looked up. "Thank you for coming."

The gremlin nodded. The pink tinge of his skin looked grayer beneath the dusting of grime.

"Vampire, we could use your help."

Though weary, Roque stood. "Let's go." He took Edeen's hand and drew her to her feet. "I need a safe place for her."

"My safe place is with you."

Roque stared at her as though he had something of great import to tell her, but instead he shook his head, and said, "You're worn-out."

"As are you."

A sad smile touched his mouth and he ran his knuckles along her cheek, before nodding.

They spent the entire day moving from house to house, Roque identifying heartbeats buried in rubble, and then the gremlins pulled survivors out.

They worked tirelessly.

Creatures of dark magic, Edeen thought. Vampires and gremlins, yet she could see no darkness in them. Nay, she witnessed nobility shored by compassion and heart.

Everything she thought she knew about magic and their dark and light properties was crushed beneath the seeking hands of a few gremlins.

They worked late into the day, taking small breaks where sandwiches and warm tea were offered from the back of a lorry to all the rescue workers.

Edeen helped as best she could, mainly soothing victims through use of her errant gift, guiding their memories to happier times. Though her gift was sporadic, she still remained a calming influence and the gremlins quickly learned to bring her in to help immediately, while Roque sometimes went on ahead to find the next heartbeat.

She met him on the street, walking toward her, a young girl in his arms. Something had changed.

The gremlins with him walked with a slower gait, less urgent, weariness bowing their shoulders.

Edeen hurried toward them, heedless of the cuts on her feet. "The child?"

"She's alive," Roque said, not meeting her gaze.

She looked to one of the gremlins.

Frowning, he slid his helmet off his bald head. "There were two pulses when we began."

The press of tears burned behind Edeen's eyes and

in her throat. Even with all they'd saved, losing one... She shook her head.

"We've searched all the houses," the gremlin said. "We need to get this one to the Infirmary."

Roque's gaze lifted. "I'd like to take her."

The gremlin nodded. "I'll show you the way."

Chapter Fifteen

The Royal Infirmary was a bustle of activity. It reminded Edeen of the activity within their keep after a long hunt. Women and men in white clothing or faded green uniforms directed injured to different areas of the building or loved ones to where they could wait for news. No body stood still. All looked tired and bewildered.

Seeing the child in Roque's arms, a woman in a white dress and a crisp hat sliding off dark hair rushed over, calling out to two men in uniforms to bring over a little padded cart on wheels.

When the girl had been settled, Edeen looked up at the woman and gasped. "Charity."

The woman blinked at her as she tiredly pushed back loose strands off her hair that had come out of her bun. She looked so much like Charity, Edeen was stunned into silence.

"We'll take good care of her. Is she yours?"

Edeen didn't answer. The events of the day and now this were wearing on her.

"No," Roque filled in. "We found her in a fallen house. Her mother was dead beside her."

The woman blanched but quickly recovered, steeling her spine and nodded. Her gaze lowered to Edeen's bare feet.

"Come with me. There's a bit of a loll. Let me see what you've done to yourself."

Roque followed her gaze down and it seemed as though the life the past hours had sucked from him flooded back. "My gods. Edeen, I didn't think..."

She took his hand. "'Tis only cuts and bruising. There were more urgent concerns."

Roque's frown suggested he wasn't going to take her absolution so easily.

"Come," the woman beckoned, but before Edeen could take one step, Roque swept her up into his arms.

"I'm sorry," he whispered. "I should have realized."

Nay, he was definitely not going to let it go. "What is this place? A convent?"

"A con--?" He looked around at all the women scurrying about in the same white dresses and crisp headwear and smiled. 'Twas good to see and filled her with a different kind of warmth than what his dragon fire provided.

"This is a place of healing. Those women are all nurses." His forehead drew tight. "The doctors, I guess, are all occupied."

The *nurse* took them to a small cluttered room with a desk of metal where Roque settled her into a wooden slatted chair. The nurse got right to business, kneeling and taking Edeen's foot in her palms. Her manner was so like Charity's, Edeen stared at the top of her head.

The nurse swabbed the worst of the cuts with puffed linen and some substance that stung, yet Edeen felt the trace stirrings of a healing, though the nurse acted as though naught was happening.

"Ye're a Healer Sorceress?"

The woman's head snapped up so abruptly 'twas a wonder her head remained attached. Her eyes were wide as though her healing ability was a deep secret.

Edeen wrinkled her brow. 'Twas a place devoted to healing, was it not? "Should there not be healers here?"

The nurse gave her a wry look-over. "None in our family has been called Healer Sorceress for a long time." She stared at Edeen a while longer, taking her measure and then glanced up at Roque to find confirmation of what she must suspect.

Edeen was not sure what passed between them. She was lost in the subtleties of what could be spoken of magic and what could not here. Gremlins and vampires were accepted easily, yet apparently a healer needed to keep her skills hidden.

Mayhap it had to do with Hitler seeking magical wielders for his own dark purposes. A group of ghouls or gremlins had a chance of withstanding soldiers. A healer alone did not.

Her feet tingled as a flow of magic reknit the flesh around the worst of the wounds.

The nurse's forehead was tight. Shadows smudged beneath her eyes. "I've taken care of the worse. The rest will heal on their own. My gift isn't so strong as others, and I'm trying to help as many as I can, though..." Her skin grayed, showing a glimpse of the despair she held back by a tenuous thread. ". . . there's so many."

Edeen reached down and took her hand. "Thank you. I'm sure whatever ye're able to do for any of them makes a difference."

She nodded. "I just wish I had more to give." She frowned before looking up at Edeen. "Just so you know, I felt your gift. I sense what you are, and..." Her tone filled with wonder. "Your abilities are intact, resting beneath the surface, but they will come back to you fully restored. I'm sure of it."

Edeen's heart leaped inside her ribcage. She blinked back sudden tears and felt Roque's hand curl over her shoulder. Unable to speak, Edeen squeezed the woman's hand and nodded.

The nurse squeezed back, her voice awed. "Who are you? There are no more empaths."

Edeen strained around her vocal chords to answer. "Edeen, just Edeen." *Last empath in the world, once guardian of the Fae's magic that she failed to protect.*

The nurse's knowing gaze was penetrating, but she

didn't push further, and instead gave her a wan smile. "Well, Edeen, then. I'm Judith. If you wait, I have a pair of shoes you're welcome to."

Edeen dropped her gaze to her bare toes. They already felt much better. "I appreciate that."

Judith rubbed her shoulders, clearly aching. "I'll get them. I just need to check on a patient first. Poor lad was plucked from the Firth this morning, near frozen."

Heat flared off Roque, shimmering along his skin. "What?" He grabbed Judith by her arms, pulling her to her feet. "This man . . . take us to him at once."

Shocked at his sudden reaction, Judith led them out the door and into the over-filled hallway once more. The atmosphere was more subdued than before. The majority of people lining the walls looked tired and in differing stages of grief and disbelief.

Without warning, Roque swung around and lifted Edeen into his arms. His features were so pinched with his own worry, she didn't complain.

Judith took them into another long hallway with many beds, all occupied, with thin draperies separating them.

Nurses and men in thin white coats bustled about them. They followed Judith to the farthest bed in the room.

Moving past the draperies, Edeen gasped. Roque's chest moved in a huge exhalation against her.

"Alex, thank the gods."

Judith went immediately to the young man and lifted

his wrist to find his pulse. He was pale, his face badly bruised. Anger flashed through Edeen at the beating he'd taken.

"He's too cold." Judith lifted the thin white coverlet and pulled out two clear bags filled with water. "These have gone cold." Anger stained her cheeks and once again Edeen was struck by her uncanny resemblance to Charity. They even shared the same mannerisms.

"I've been using my ability throughout the day to get his body core temperature up." Judith placed the bags aside. "Even with these, it hasn't been enough. I'll have to reheat the water." She looked at the slumbering young man with apology. "We're understaffed for what we're dealing with, yet he shouldn't have been left unattended so long. My fault." She brushed a loose strand of hair back. "There was a child—"

Roque let Edeen down and went to Judith. His voice was gentle. "It's all right. What can we do now? What does Alex need?"

"Alex?" Judith's gaze lifted, then settled back on her charge. A tiny smile drifted over her lips. "Suits him." And then she straightened. "We need to get his temperature up . . . from the inside. These water bags are cooling too fast and my magic . . ."

Roque nudged her gently aside. "*This* I can do." He placed his palms upon Alex's chest. After a moment, drifts of steam rose from Roque's skin to swirl in the air.

Judith pulled the draperies closed.

Edeen took Alex's limp hand in hers. 'Twas frighteningly cold.

Judith took out a strange devise which she placed in her ears and the single end onto Alex's chest, moving it a bit until she seemed satisfied she had it in the right place. "His breathing is better." She took his other wrist. "He's warmer already." She eyed Roque. "Whatever you're doing, keep doing it."

Roque nodded curtly, drops of perspiration pooling across his brow.

And a miracle happened. Alex stirred.

They all inhaled a collective breath, waiting.

"Alex." Edeen pushed his hair back from his poor battered face. "Alex, can ye hear me?"

"Mmmmm," he hummed and Judith and Edeen smiled across the bed at each other.

"Alex, can you open your eyes and let us know you're with us?" Judith coaxed.

His head turned, responding to her voice and one eye opened, the other too swollen, and blinked up at Judith. A bemused smile tugged at the corner of his cut lips until Roque startled him out of it. "Alex."

Alex jerked his gaze to Roque, his features twisting with pain. "Cor. I awoke to beauty, but now here's your ugly mug."

"Very amusing," Roque said blandly, yet his eyes

shone. "Bloody hell, Alex, don't do that again."

"All right. What did I do?" A trace of a smile warmed his weary gaze.

"Let yourself get tossed into the Firth."

Alex's eye's closed and he nodded. "Ah, right. That wasn't one of my best plans. I'll avoid poking at trolls in the future."

Judith patted his arm, drawing his attention back to her and Alex's countenance once again fell into a bemused state like he couldn't quite grasp if she were real or not.

"Go back to sleep," she said. "You need to regain your strength."

He nodded, watching her every move. Amusement curled Edeen's lips. Alex had refused her offer to help with his burned hands, yet he readily gave into Judith.

Edeen looked from one to the other, noting the slight rosiness to Judith's cheeks and how her mannerisms were suddenly off, somewhat self-conscious.

Judith glanced at Alex, then away, and tried pushing her stray hair back inside her bun. "I've got to go. There's others needing my attention."

Roque reached over Alex and took Judith's arm to stop her. "Thank you. For all you've done for him."

Judith nodded and ducked away.

Alex gave a low whistle. "Damn, Roque. Think you can leave me alone with the pretty nurse next time?"

Roque jabbed a finger at him. "There better not be a next time. Alex, I'm—"

Alex held up a hand. "Don't say it. I'm fine."

"You're beat to hell."

Alex shrugged, then winced. "Point is, we're all safe." His gaze slid to Edeen. He couldn't have missed their dirty and disheveled appearance. "Roque, what the hell happened?"

Alex's face turned grayer and grayer as Roque filled him in on the events of the day.

Chapter Sixteen

She awoke to the soft murmur of voices. She sat in a hard chair, body leaning against the side of Alex's thin bed. She didn't remember being in a chair, nor falling asleep. A pair of women's black brogues without cross laces, were on the floor next to her feet.

The voices stopped talking as she opened her eyes and found Roque and Alex both looking at her. The lanterns were low, the heavy black fabric had been lowered to cover all the windows, which subdued any moonlight that might have come in.

Somewhere Roque had found himself a shirt.

She smiled at Alex's appearance. Though still swollen and bruised, his pallor was much better. He sat up against a pillow and she could see that his arm was encased in layers of wrappings. Relief swarmed through her and something else . . . a quiet tenderness she'd before only reserved for her brothers.

"Ye look better. Are ye all right, Alex?"

"They tell me I'll live." He grinned. "What of you, Edeen? You look near done in."

She felt it in every joint and muscle. "I'll keep."

Roque looked at her with something akin to pride shining in his eyes, making strange little prickles leap around in her belly.

Judith pushed aside the drapery. "I've asked around for you and found out the train station wasn't hit. There's only one train leaving for Glasgow at dawn, but there's many trying to be on it. You're best chance is to be at the station tonight."

Roque rubbed his temple, the weariness taking its toll. Had he rested at all while she slept? Vampire, dragon, or nay, he had to take care of himself.

He needed someone to see to it. Edeen's heart flinched at the realization she wanted to be that person.

Roque's hand had moved to his forehead, pressing in. "I've lost all track of time." He smiled apologetically.

"It's a little before midnight," Judith informed.

Alex made to swing his legs off the mattress. Stepping agilely to the side of the bed, Judith stopped his progress, putting a hand to his chest. "You aren't going anywhere."

"Of course I am." Alex's scowl reeked of defiance. "Don't tell me you don't need the bed."

"We don't need the bed." Judith's stern look suggested Alex wasn't going to win the argument.

"She's right, Alex," Edeen patted his bandaged arm. "Please rest and get better."

He looked from Edeen to Judith and threw up his

uninjured arm in defeat. "Oh bother, it's not fair, the two of you ganging up on me."

"Never stood a chance, mate." Roque chuckled. He leaned close to Alex and grasped his forearm. "Stay here, regain your strength . . . and flirt with the pretty nurse. You can thank me later."

Alex's eyes slid over to Judith who busily began folding bandages on the tray, pretending not to hear. "Well, when you put it that way . . ." Alex gripped Roque's arm tighter, his features taking on a seriousness rarely betrayed. "Hey, be careful."

Roque grinned. "You know me."

"That's what I'm afraid of." He looked away. "Watch out for Edeen."

Roque's grin dropped. "*That* you can count on."

Edeen rolled her eyes. They were worse than her brothers, and like when her brothers became overly protective, a tender place in her heart warmed. She slipped on the shoes and went to Alex, cupped his face between her palms and kissed him. "Thank you, Alex. For everything."

She wanted to say more, but couldn't think of how, but the warmth in his expression relayed that he already knew how she felt.

Roque turned to Judith. "See that he stays out of trouble."

"I will."

Then as an afterthought, he said, "If anyone tries to kick him out of this bed, inform them he's a lieutenant in Her Majesties Royal Army, attaché to the Ministry of Defense. Lieutenant Alexander Greves."

The air rushed out of Edeen's lungs.

"I'm Charity Greves from Seattle."

Col's lips twisted and Edeen forced back a smile. "That's quite the telling. Ye're from centuries beyond us? And ye believed ye could simply travel back here and pluck my brother out from under the grasp of the most fearsome witch of a hundred generations?"

Edeen looked from Alex to Judith, a strange floaty sensation cresting over her essence as Roque guided her from the partitioned room.

Chapter Seventeen

She wanted to check on Margaret and Thomas and after all Edeen had lost, Roque wouldn't deny her anything.

His heart squeezed, watching her with the children, giving them reassurances, praising their courage. Her face crumpled when they asked if the *Luftwaffe* would come back. Edeen didn't coddle, but told them she didn't know. She kissed each head and left the children to the Infirmary's care.

They walked along the silent streets, neither felt like talking. The full moon cast eerie light upon battered shells of buildings as well as entire blocks that had been left untouched.

Late, there were very few people out, most hunkered down in railway tunnels or spending the night within their pre-fabricated Anderson shelters. A few Air Raid Protection wardens were out, some of the gremlins they'd worked with earlier remained on the streets, casting wary glances up at the sky.

Edeen stumbled and Roque caught her elbow, aware that she didn't share his or the gremlins' keen eyesight and with the black materials covering all windows and doors and dull black tape covering every reflective surface from iron trim on the unlit street lamps to the shine of bicycle bells, even in the moonlight, she'd have trouble seeing obstacles.

At least she had on some damn shoes. Guilt rose in Roque's chest over that.

He took her hand in his, moving onto Bakers Brae toward the rail station. The sooner he ensconced her in Glasgow, the better.

Then what?

He wasn't simply going to deliver her to the powers-that-be, that was for damn certain. She would not be a pawn or weapon, even for the Allies. Military Intelligence could decipher their own bleeding codes.

She was under his protection now. He'd take her to his mother's people if he had to.

An entire coven of vampires could bloody well keep her safe.

Or they could go to the Americans, though he doubted the yanks would remain neutral in this war much longer. Roque squeezed her hand. Whatever they did, he wasn't leaving her.

Mate, the dragon purred and Roque didn't push the thought aside. Whatever this was between them, this pull, he was utterly hers.

He stopped and took both her hands. Her expressive

face angled up toward his.

"Edeen . . . ?"

Her pulse pounded a rhythm straight to his heart, steady and strong, like she was. His blood burned to take her. Fire exploded in his belly, radiating through him. His palm dragged into her hair, cupped the back of her head and brought her to him. Warm lips pressed to cool lips and the world tilted, spinning away. Fire blanketed his soul, threatening to burn, burn, yet his focus filed down to Edeen, her lips, her soft skin, giving everything she was to him and the dragon cooled, pacified, enthralled by the woman's touch. Her taste. Her smell. *Mate*. *His*. *Treasure*. The serpent would never touch her in flame.

Roque nearly wept with the miracle of Edeen.

And an air raid siren pierced the quiet. The world tilted back to reality.

Frozen, they jerked their gazes to the sky.

The first bombs dropped. The heavy stuttering drone of planes boomed overhead. The sky grew red. Up the street, the Ardgowan Distillery took a direct hit. The ground vibrated through the soles of their shoes and incendiary bombs dropped like glittering streamers of light in the black sky. More booms and blossoms of red.

Wine from the distillery ran down the street on fire—a bright beacon for the planes searching out targets. With this much flame, the pilots most likely believed they hit on something huge, like the gasworks or shipyards.

"We have to get off this street!" Roque practically yanked Edeen into moving. Liquid fire lashed out at their heels. Not fast enough, Roque scooped Edeen up and soared like the dragon he was, feet barely slapping on the pavement.

Anti-artillery whistled into the sky. Search lights swept dark underbellies of planes, wave after wave. There were hundreds.

An incendiary bomb slammed down ahead of them, spouting fire, ready to catch on anything that burned.

Setting Edeen down on the run, Roque dove over it, slapping out flames with his hands. The sleeves of his shirt caught on fire.

"Roque!" Edeen screamed for him, a knife of fear he hadn't heard in her tone before.

He spun just as a claw lashed out at him.

Already low, Roque rolled to his shoulder and came up swinging.

Geschopf was here? How was Geschopf here?

Wulf took the hit, staggering back.

Air whooshed behind him and there were twin thuds. Roque felt the much slower pulses of vampires as they dropped from the church roof behind him.

Another dropped near Edeen and a fourth strolled out from behind the burning distillery.

Geschopf smiled and Roque was a vulnerable child again, heart squeezed so tight in his chest that it would tear out of his ribcage.

Geschopf stepped toward him. "I will always—"

Roque didn't give him a chance to finish, but instead swirled, slamming the side of his arm into the closest vampire's throat. He dropped like a stone and the second vampire flew into Roque, hauling him backwards, feet dragging across pavement until he slammed into a wall. His head rocked forward and the vampire started pounding his chest. Face. Ribs.

Growling, Roque struck back. Up under the chin, another to the belly. Grabbing the vamp's head, he twisted, kicking his feet out from under him and the vampire twisted in a grotesque somersault. A close explosion ripped him off his feet. A building a street over, sugar factory, exploded. Flames flashed in all directions, orange and blue. Burning sugar.

On his stomach, Roque shook his head, disoriented. He heard Edeen screaming his name. He pulled to his hands and knees.

Geschopf was also rousing. Still on their feet, the vampires held Edeen between them. She struggled frantically.

Fury roared through his veins.

He lunged up to take back what was his.

Geschopf leapt in his way, shoving so hard, Roque flew back, hitting the ground with jarring force.

"Take the girl to the boat," Wulf barked out. His eyes

reflected gold in the light of the burning city. "I'll see to this one."

Roque came off the ground like a sprinter, lunging after the vampires dragging Edeen away.

Something slammed into his side, sliding him across the ground. The blond vampire again.

They took Edeen.

He didn't have time for this. He kicked, he punched, he let his fury fire every hit. Flames erupted across his skin. Someone was screaming, the vampire? Trying to get away, but Roque was beyond mercy.

"Yes, yes!" Geschopf's voice echoed as though in a hollow cave. "This is who you are, what I have made you. Extraordinary. Powerful."

Roque stopped, shocked. The unconscious vampire hung limp in his bloody hands, clothes on fire, blond hair singed to blackness.

"No," Roque gritted out and dropped the vampire to the ground. He squelched his flames out. "No."

"You're a magnificent creature, Roquemore. Unique to the world. Do not waste what you are."

Roque grunted, and looked down at the burning vampire. "To destroy? Is that the summation of a creature's worth?"

Geschopf raised his fist. A vein bulged in his forehead. "To live fully! I've given you a divine purpose, Roquemore—the control to tap into your full potential. You

145

have strength and power never before known. Cease holding back. Embrace the dragon!"

"For you?" Roque straightened to his full height, hatred for this man, this monster, flaring, boiling heat in his stomach.

Fire danced behind Geschopf, casting his wide arrogant stance in orange and reds. Roque turned away, no longer a young boy, no longer afraid.

"Roquemore!" *Die Schwarze Klaue* roared. An eerie sound crackled across the air, like the scraping of scales dragging across bark.

Roque twisted back.

Bones. The reshaping of bones and muscle. Geschopf's flesh was tearing apart, blood and sinew dripping in soupy ropes as scales, shiny and slick emerged. Clothes burst at the seams, unable to hold the growing mass of muscle and chest.

Wings unfurled.

Roque stared into the lengthening snout and glittering golden eye just before the dragon launched at him.

Chapter Eighteen

The world was noise and flame. Edeen pulled against the vampires dragging her from Roque. Their grips on her arms were too strong. She screamed at them, stomped on their feet.

One of those small bombs meant to catch things on fire dropped several yards away, immediately sprouting flame.

Jerking, one of the vampires loosened his hold and Edeen yanked her arm free, raising it to his chest.

The other grabbed her arm and twisted it behind her back.

"*Nein*, none of that, *Fräulein*." Cold breath whispered across her ear.

The vampire facing her looked from his chest and back to her. His lips rolled back in a snarl, pulling away from sharp incisors. A feral gleam shot thought his gaze.

A bomb dropped directly onto his head, throwing Edeen and her captor back. He burst into flame.

Fire blazed off the fallen vampire.

Dazed, Edeen lay on her back, across the other vampire.

Bleeding hells. Rolling off him, she scrambled to her feet and ran.

In a blur, the vampire cut her off, grabbing her arm as he jerked to a stop.

There was a sharp crack and she nearly went blind with pain. Her own scream echoed distantly in her head. Her arm, her arm.

Vision clearing, she lifted her face to the vampire. He looked as shocked at what he'd done as she was.

And Edeen risked the opportunity, slamming her palm and her essence into his chest.

They both went rigid.

Her gift was a chaotic riot, streaming through the man's emotions like a runaway steed.

Edeen felt herself whimper, pain erupted behind her eyes.

Fierce images and emotions rammed into her, powerful, ugly, enhanced by hate and fear. Torture. Geschopf's laughter as the Black Claw abused this vampire, as he had Roque, creating an army of obedient unquestioning supercharged magical soldiers. Geschopf's techniques were gruesome, brutal, punching into Edeen. She had to get control of her gift or 'twould be her who was lost to this terror.

Judith said the fullness of her gift was just beneath the surface. . . .

With all that she was and ever had been . . .

daughter, sister, guardian . . . empath, Edeen went deep, reaching for her gift, seeking the flow of essence uniquely hers.

As she pulled back into herself, she felt the vampire push, ripping her out of his memories. He was strong, fighting for his life as well as Geschopf's cause. Geschopf, his torturer, as loyal and obedient to him as a beaten dog to its master.

Pride swelled within her that Roque, having endured more from Geschopf than this vampire, had not let himself be destroyed.

The Black Claw had not broken Roque's spirit.

Neither would she be broken.

Her gift pulsed before her, wild and unleashed, whipping out like streaks of flaring lightning, dangerous and lethal.

The vampire pushed her to the edge, strengthening.

...and Edeen soared, shot her essence to her core and grabbed onto her gift. Hers.

She held on, taming, pulling, and guided it back to the vampire and his horrendous fears. She shied from them, and then lowered her head and pressed on, sifting through the awful, awful tortures until she found one to use.

Geschopf was a monster.

Vampires healed so the *Die Schwarzen Klaue* took advantage of that healing ability, and performed monstrosities other creatures could not live through. As the vampire's intestines were cut out, Edeen guided him there, locking him within that moment, leaving his mind trapped there, and quietly slipped away.

Her hand dropped away and she was once again in the burning street, chest heaving raggedly. The vampire rolled on the ground, screaming, clawing at his stomach.

Edeen's mouth went dry at what she had done. She didn't know how long he would be trapped there or if he'd remain in the memory forever. She'd never done anything like this before.

She stiffened her shoulders and pulled her broken arm to her stomach. She couldn't think on that now. She had to get back to Roque.

Chapter Nineteen

She raced through the streets, dodging burning shells of buildings. A bomb hit a home in front of her, blasting out windows. Glass shot out in all directions like crystal arrows. Edeen dropped to the ground. A chair slid across her legs and continued rolling.

Lunging up, Edeen kept going, trying to find her way through the changing maze of the broken streets. Dark shadows of the flying machines groaned above her, filling the sky with glittering trailing lights. Streaks of brightness whistled up to meet them.

An otherworldly shriek rang out, penetrating her chest. Edeen froze, before veering toward the direction it came, scrabbling over fallen masonry, clutching her broken arm tight to herself and came upon a scene of nightmare and legend.

Dragon.

Within a shell of a church, a dragon shrieked, red muscular neck craned upward in triumph. Orange flames licked across red shiny scales. His claws and scales midway up his forelegs shone black.

'Twas a smaller dragon than those depicted on

tapestries, barely larger than the height of a man, but wreathed in crimson muscle and an impenetrable hide.

A man, also on fire, pushed up from the broken floor, lunging at the dragon and was batted away by a great wing, to roll in the air.

"Roque!"

The dragon's head flicked to her, long leathery wings expanding.

"Noooo!" Roque roared, leaping at the beast.

A black claw swiped down, thrusting Roque to the ground.

Screaming, Edeen climbed over debris, trying to get into that church. Geschopf lifted Roque in his claws, twisting his body. He was going to break his spine. Tears streamed over Edeen's vision. *Nay. Nay!.* This was not happening. Not to Roque. Not Roque.

Roque exploded in a showering fountain of energy and light, lifting Edeen off her feet. She hit the ground, wrenching her arm.

The church spun sideways in her vision. Everything went suddenly quiet. Dust and ash floated around her in a motion too slow to be real and then abruptly everything crashed back into harsh sound and movement.

From the church, a green dragon lifted into the air, shrieking, trumpeting a challenge.

Oh gods, Roque.

He was beautiful.

Wings sweeping wide, Roque shot off. Shrieking in fury.

The red dragon expanded his wings like a boast. Jaws widening, he screeched out in triumph. 'Twas what he'd wanted all along, for Roque to embrace his dragon.

Edeen's heart pounded. What if Roque...what if he lost himself to this?

Bunching his muscles, Geschopf leaped into the air, giving chase.

The dragons streaked over the city, into the *Luftwaffe*. Planes veered out of their path.

Lights from the ground swept over them. Whistling missiles shot upward.

The dragons crashed into each other, claws locked, spinning, falling through the air. Wind howled through their wings.

Edeen ran to keep them in sight, losing them behind houses and buildings. She found them again, winging back this way, the green dragon had the red on the run.

Geschopf shouldered into a plane. It sputtered and fell from the sky, streaking toward Roque.

Edeen froze, heart hammering, afraid, as Roque banked away beneath the guttering plane and righted himself to soar after the red.

They came together again, rolling, rolling, spiraling toward the earth.

Their shrieks filled the air, pitching over explosions

and drones of aircraft.

The green dragon hissed, jaws sprouting flame and a plane erupted in flame and fell from the sky, a sputtering roar, coughing from its tail end with billowing smoke.

Edeen watched in horror, afraid that Roque didn't know what he was doing, didn't care that swiping planes from the sky would fall cause as much damage to the city as the bombs the planes dropped. She clamped her injured arm to herself tight, shaking. What if Geschopf was right? What if Roque was already lost?

The red's jaws clamped over Roque's long neck and he screamed, wings beating the air, pulling all their weight skyward, harder, harder.

Into the midst of the planes, straight into the path of a large bomber. He wrenched free...

The plane crashed point on into the red dragon, exploding on impact. Plane and dragon erupted into a fiery ball of light, trailing smoke and large chunks of falling debris. Geschopf beat his fiery wings, trying to launch higher in the air, but he was burning, burning, from the inside. Flames radiated through the center of his belly and his hide, sprouting arcs of fire that shot out onto aircraft trying to veer around him. His wings stroked furiously up and down in an attempt to pull himself upward, but it was too late. Flame whisked across wings, ruining skin and hide, making them glow in the dark sky, until they were useless burning leather that supported him no more. He rolled, spiraling through the air, crashing into planes that smoked and dove out of the sky, screeching in their fatal descents, until Geschopf, completely on fire, shrieked through the air like a whistling comet, dragging clouds of smoke . . . until all at once, he exploded in a giant concussion of fire and then was no more.

Chunks of ash, and Edeen didn't want to consider what else, floated from the sky like burning hail stones.

But where was Roque? She searched the sky, following the beams from the searchlights, until . . . there? Nay. A plane screeched past. She swallowed, craning her neck. The smoke and soot hurt her eyes, but still she scanned the skies, and...the green dragon shot across two buildings, wings on fire, streaking fast toward the ground.

Nay, Roque. Heart in her throat, Edeen ran, trying to keep him in sight. He was close, coming so close, falling fast.

She rounded a corner, blocked off by a river of burning liquid and Air Raid Protection men, some gremlins, working to put it out.

She fled down another street, flying out from behind another home, mostly intact, in time to see Roque lose his transformation, change back into a man, and drop behind a broken building.

He'd never withstand a fall that far. No one could. *Vampires heal, vampires heal,* her mind screamed.

Please, please be all right.

She skidded into the broken square she thought he had dropped into. The contents of the large building were on fire. Rolls of tapestries or heavy draperies burned…she didn't care.

"Roque!"

Dropping her broken arm to hang painfully at her side, she began rifling through debris, frantic to find him.

A soft exhalation raised the hairs along her arms.

She spun.

She scrambled down into a small crater.

And her heart came to a screeching stop.

Roque was there. Gods, he was there, laying on his side, facing away from her, one arm stretched back behind him, clothes burned away.

"Roque," she whispered, afraid and climbed down beside him.

He was so still, smoldering and bleeding. With the use of only one arm, she lifted his head and scooted her knee beneath him.

"Roque." She patted his cheek, laid her palm above his heart and waited for his chest to rise. She nearly wept with relief when he inhaled.

"Oh, Roque." *Please let him be himself. Please let him come back to her.* She curled over his head as though the closeness could will him back to consciousness. His dark lashes fluttered, and then stilled.

The planes continued to drone overhead, dropping bombs, a never-ending barrage. Edeen lifted her head at the sound of rock scraping on pavement.

"Over here. Help us! Please."

A shadow moved out of the dark, coming toward them, then stepped into the glowing reflection of the building's fire.

Every muscle in Edeen's body tightened.

The vampire, the one who broke her arm and who she had left locked in his torturous memories, sneered. His fists clenched. Blood coated his stomach. Madness twisted his features.

"I'll help you, bitch. I'm going to snap your other arm and then your pretty little neck."

A blur dove between them. More hazy shapes drew out of the night. The gremlin wardens surrounded the vampire.

One of them spoke, "Not here, not on Scotland soil, ye don't. Ye filthy, dirty krout."

As one, the gremlins swarmed over him.

Chapter Twenty

Roque awoke to the pulse of hundreds of heartbeats along with the soft murmur of voices and the scuffling of footsteps. The scent of blood hung heavy in the air tinged with sharp ammonia and the sweet odor of morphine.

Hospital or Infirmary then. Fighting to lift his heavy eyelids, he searched for the one heartbeat among the others that had become his lifeline, and sighed in sudden contentment when he found her, close and calm.

It picked up at his sigh. "Roque?" A soft hand slid onto his cheek. "Are ye awakening?"

Gods, yes. Would that he forever awakened to this. He turned toward her voice, still fighting the battle his eyelids waged against him. He finally won, cracking his eyes open to the most beautiful sight.

"There you are." Eyes shimmery with moisture, Edeen smiled and the dragon's heart stirred. *Treasure*, it sang. And Roque wholeheartedly agreed.

"You're you, aye? Ye know me? Please say ye know me."

"I know you. My heart knows you." He smiled. "Treasure."

The tears she tried holding back spilled and she nodded, dark lashes blinking furiously.

He tried to shift up, but Edeen stopped him. "Ye're healing on yer own, but 'tis slow." She wiped her cheeks with the back of her hand, and smiled weakly, the shadows beneath her eyes revealing her worry. "Mayhap dragons do not heal as swiftly as vampires."

Roque jolted, remembering the transformation, sparing in the skies, bellowing a challenge to Geschopf." Every muscle in his body tightened. He had transformed. He squeezed his eyes shut, remembering the wind whisking across his body, the powerful thrust of wings pulling him through the sky. He had transformed. And he was still himself. Geschopf had been wrong. He did not lose himself. He was who he was, dragon, vampire, or man.

An upwelling of peace poured through his soul, touching the heat and magic inside him. The dragon stretched, spreading his wings, relishing freedom. He'd never felt more alive. Roque opened his eyes.

Edeen frowned, studying him.

His smile broadened. "I'm well. All's well." He thought of the burning red dragon spiraling through the sky. "Geschopf?"

"Gone. Dead. The planes have also left." She glanced forlornly past the gap in the drawn curtain. "All is quiet."

Roque nodded. He would not mourn the death of *Die Schwarzen Klaue*, though he did not like the sadness touching Edeen's features. He looked her over, stiffening at the sling holding her arm to her chest. "You're hurt."

She looked down at the wrappings on her arm. "A clean break. Judith offered to help it mend, but she's so tired . . ."

Roque reached for her other hand, sensing a great sorrow. "What is it? What's wrong?"

Liquid eyes met his and she shrugged her feelings off as unimportant.

"Edeen?"

She tore her gaze away and Roque felt bereft of her contact. "'Tis this world. In my heart, I feel it is not right. 'Tis not meant to be this way. My brothers . . . Shaw was never meant to unbalance the magic of the world . . . yet, I also see light, so much light even amid darkness."

"My magic is dark, Edeen."

"Aye! As is the gremlins and the ghouls. Yet I see no darkness in yer souls. Magic has changed, blended, and that seems right to me."

"Yet . . ." he prodded.

"My core instincts say otherwise...that Shaw, that my brothers . . . their fate was not meant to be. I'm sure of it."

"You grieve for them." Roque rubbed his thumb along her wrist. "There's no going back in time. Nothing you can do."

Her gaze swept to his, imploring him to understand. "I've attempted to pen a missive." She slid her hand from his and took a sheet of paper from the little metal night stand.

His brows rose, seeing the little paragraph of unfamiliar runes, and his heart went out to how much she had lost, and how much she had yet to learn about this century. "Is that Gaelic?"

Edeen nodded. "Alex spoke of codes." She shrugged. "I cannot leave this for just anyone."

A troubling thought niggled at the corner of his mind. "Who? Who can you leave the letter for? Who do you know who can possibly read Gaelic?"

"Charity. The Healer Sorceress of the future. Her grandmother insisted—will insist—that she learn ancient languages. Her grandmother, Judith Greves."

And the bottom dropped out of his world. He swallowed, shell-shocked. It could work. It could change everything. If Edeen warned Charity not to travel back to the Thirteenth Century, Toren, the High Sorcerer, would not be rescued from the witch. Shaw would take the guardian clan and its magic into the Shadowrood, but he would also not remain on the earth to unbalance magic to darkness.

And Edeen would not be sent into a seven hundred year slumber

Roque's throat closed up. "Edeen, if history is altered,

we will never meet."

There was every possibility that he might not even be born with dark magic not as rampant. With dark magic not awakening dragons from their millennial slumbers to mate with mankind. Or his vampire mother.

A tear leaked onto her cheek. "I know." She tilted a corner of her letter for him to see. "'Tis why I cannot finish. Oh, Roque, I cannot bear a world without you in it. I cannot." She flung herself in his arms, openly weeping. "I do not know what to do."

Holding her to him, he smoothed his palm down her hair. "Shh, it's all right, love. Everything will work out how it should."

She lifted her tear-stained face, and his heart ached for her. "But I want to stay here. I w-want to help Alex break the c-codes and stop Hitler. I want to stay with you."

Keep her, the dragon stirred. *Never let her go.*

Roque kissed her hard and for a moment everything floated away. It was just them in any realm. They were meant to be together. He placed his trust in that.

His trust in her.

He pulled back, staring hard to memorize every precious inflection to her features.

"Write your letter, Edeen. We'll leave it in the hands of fate."

~~~

Trembling and heart sore, Edeen walked through the long hall to Alex's bed, a sealed envelope clutched in her shaking hand.

Judith was just stepping past the drapery, a vibrant blush to her cheeks. Beyond her shoulder, Alex caught sight of Edeen and flashed her an unrepentant grin.

Heart heavy, Edeen merely nodded back and spoke to Judith, holding out the letter. "I need yer help."

The End

On May 6, 1941, a little after midnight, fifty German planes attacked the town of Greenock, Scotland, targeting in apparent random fashion. The *Luftwaffe*, three hundred planes strong, reappeared the following night. Again, the brunt of the attack was taken mostly by civilians, leaving the Royal Navy shipyards relatively untouched. Two-hundred-eighty people were killed with twelve thousand left injured.

Although I took liberty with some of the events, the distilleries and sugar factory were hit.

However, to my knowledge, there were no sightings of gremlins, trolls, vampires, or dragons.

I hope you enjoyed my little romp back and forth through time. Please don't worry about Shaw and Col. The boys each get their own adventure in time-travel until all the sibling guardians reunite together for the conclusion. Find hints and extra tidbits about the characters and how magic works within the world of the Highland Sorcery novels at my blog, clovercheryl.blogspot.com. Just what is a moon sifter anyway?

Next up is Col's journey as he is thrown forward in time where he learns things are not exactly ideal for a shapeshifter on his own. Look for *Highland Shapeshifter* at your favorite book selling sites.

Excerpt from Highland Shapeshifter

Ogres stink.

There's no getting around the odor. Even with the astringent scent of angelica oil Lenore had dabbed beneath her nose, the bar reeked. She'd probably have to burn these clothes.

High tones from an elfish lyre lilted out from the scratchy speaker system, an airy enchantment squashed instantly by the musty dark atmosphere of the pub.

"In back." Gainy, Starch's right hand man, well, ogre, canted his bulbous head, displacing swirls of smoke with the movement. "Been waiting on you, Little Pix."

Lenore rolled her eyes and tucked the wayward strands of her white-blond bangs back beneath her knitted cap. "I bet he has. The shipment came early then?"

"Not exactly. Starch has something better."

"What?" Lenore whirled on the fidgety ogre, her head barely topping as high as his protruding ribcage. She jabbed a finger at him. She needed this shipment. Like yesterday. The vamps wouldn't be able to hold off the blood addiction without the *crimson tear* and she didn't even want to think about how the ifrits had been managing without larkspur this long.

She'd left in the middle of the night at Starch's first call, prepared with more than extra in payment to get her hands on the underground supplies.

"What the hell is this? I don't need something better. I need what I arranged for." Lenore sidestepped between big bad Gainy and a ghoul who was exhaling blue smoke through a clear straw shoved up a piggish snout. In her dealings with the ogres, she'd learned to not let them play her. Be decisive and only leave with what she asked for. And pay in cash. For all their gruff and burly natures, they were the slickest salesmen on the planet and she didn't want to owe them. Don Corleone had nothing on Starch.

Horse's head, her butt. Try waking up to the severed head of a phooka in your bed. Of course, that had never happened to her because she always played it straight with the godfather of warts and slime. But she'd heard...

"Tell Starch to contact me when my stuff gets here. He knows I don't want anything to do with his other dealings."

Gainy grabbed her arm, stopping her. "Oh, you'll want to see this."

Lenore glanced at the meaty brown hand encircling her entire upper arm, before pointedly glaring straight up into Gainy's triple-pupiled eyes.

He immediately let go, lifting his palms outward in the sign of surrender. They stared in a non-verbal stand-off, while the graceful notes of the lyre filmed around them.

Gainy blinked first, and Lenore felt a smug moment of triumph until his warty lip twitched. "It involves your sister."

Everything went cold. And hard.

In a flash, her fists were bunched in Gainy's collar and she'd pulled his fat head down to her level. "My sister has nothing to do with our arrangements," she hissed in his face. All the occupants in the bar went quiet.

Lenore kept Charity in the dark. Her sister had no idea where Lenore got the more hard-to-get ingredients for their herbal shop. She'd be furious if she ever found out about the risks Lenore had been taking.

"Easy." Gainy pried her hands away.

He was a lackey anyway. Fists balled, Lenore strode to the back room, and slammed open the door.

Starch had his broad back to her, taking inventory of whatever was in several large crates on the scuffed work table. He turned toward her, the protruding hairless brow bone lifted above his too-small reading glasses. "Ah, Little Pixie, excellent timing."

She wasn't in a tolerant mood. "I thought we were friends." Okay that was pushing it. "Yet you have Gainy threatening my sister?"

Starch had the audacity to look put upon. "I did no such thing." His gaze swept beyond her shoulder where Gainy had come into the storeroom behind her.

Lenore shifted to the side to keep both ogres in sight.

Starch put down the clipboard he'd been marking inventory on. "If anything, I'm looking out for you and your sister. Got a shipment in I think you'll find interesting."

Lenore's gaze tightened. "I'm listening." Her instincts screamed *get out, get out now.* Something was terribly off, but she wasn't about to back down now.

Starch snorted. "Suspicious little healer, aren't we?"

She responded with a raised finger.

Starch cackled in throaty glee. "Come on, then. It's back here."

She followed him to the rear of the storeroom, pushing past stacked crates and covered bundles that Starch had to squeeze his bulk sideways between. Gainy came up behind them.

He brought her to a lumpy tarp on the floor, wedged up between a rickety shelf and the building's water pipe that ran from floor to ceiling.

"So where is it?" she asked and something beneath the tarp moved at the sound of her voice.

Lenore flinched back. She whirled on the ogre. "What is that?" She knew Starch's business stretched into unsavory areas, but, as yet, she'd never seen any evidence that he was blatantly involved in the trafficking of magical and mythical creatures.

Her heart slammed against her rib cage. Backing away, she shook her head. "I'm out."

The creature, whatever it was beneath the tarp, jerked again, followed by a quiet moan that shot straight to her gut.

"No one's stopping you," Starch said. His round eyes

blinked. He knew he had her.

Damn her healer's heart. It was the sole reason she did business with Starch in the first place. To get the supplies necessary to help magical wielders who couldn't get help anywhere else.

Plus, she needed to know what this had to do with Charity.

Resolved, she edged forward, and dragged the heavy tarp off the creature underneath.

And stared.

It was just a man.

He sat against the sewage pipe, arms pulled behind him either tied or handcuffed. His head hung forward, dark hair obscuring his face. His jeans were ripped and loose, as was his dirty T-shirt, splattered with blood and mud. Cuts and abrasions speckled his arms and she'd guess there were more under his shirt and on his face. Fury rose up in her.

"You're into trafficking humans now?"

"Ha!" Starch flung his large hands up. "Hardly human. Shapeshifter. And a powerful one at that. Took three ghouls and a troll to subdue him and that was after they tranqed him."

"Is he still drugged?" She crouched down beside the guy, squeezing her hands into fists to hide the anger. "What'd you give him?"

She touched his arm and he flinched. Her heart went

out to him. Her instinct was to sooth, but she couldn't show any softness here. Grabbing his chin, she lifted his head.

And the world narrowed down to a pair of mossy green eyes.

Energy shot into her, buzzing across her skin in a lightning pulse. An instant familiarity burned through her, though she was certain she'd never seen him before, but there was something... Staring into his battered face, a connection rippled between them, tangent and swift and then was gone as quickly as it came.

3903823R00096

Printed in Great Britain
by Amazon.co.uk, Ltd.,
Marston Gate.